CUT AND BOUND

KATIE MATTHEWS

ISBN: 151932216X
ISBN-13: 978-1519322166

For T.M.R.

1 UNDERNEATH

I have lived a good life, I believe. I think my thirty-seven years on this earth have been well spent. If someone asked me if I had any regrets, my immediate answer would be no.

Wouldn't it?

I mentally go through a list of accomplishments in my life: Ran my first marathon in high school. Got into Stanford and graduated magna cum laude. Worked in Silicon Valley for several years after college and then landed a position at a Fortune 500 company in Chicago and worked my way up to financial analyst, then CFO in seven years. OK, for that last one I can fairly pat myself on the back, give a cocky grin, and order the outrageously expensive Bordeaux without flinching. And I do, often.

I drive a brand-new Mercedes SL550 Roadster right up to the valet in my downtown residence building and enjoy the view from my thirtieth-floor loft. I buy women expensive dinners and presents all in the name of sex, have an amazing art collection, and have bedded many of Chicago's wealthy socialites—and several of

New York's. I bought my parents a house outside the city where they could retire. They said they wanted to stay in the city, but it's better this way. I can't have them dropping by all the time. I have visited eighteen countries and currently speak three languages. I have everything I need, or if I find something I need I can buy it. No regrets here. That's a good life, right? Hell yes, that's right.

The truth is, I have too much time to think. It's quiet and dark here, and I'm comfortable and warm. It seems that all I have is time. I have plenty of time to replay the film reel of my life and kick myself for not getting that blonde's number at that benefit last week. But I don't mind having this time for thinking, as long as this wonderful warmth stays around me. It feels like being wrapped in a feather bed, a bed of feathers, a feather burrito. Like when you're bundled up in the covers in wintertime except that even my nose sticking outside the covers is warm. The beeping of the machines is my only complaint. The annoying high pitch interferes with my reminiscing. I'm not sure why, but I think I'm in a coma.

2 THE SPACE BETWEEN BLACK AND WHITE

I'm quite sure that I'm not dead because I can breathe and hear, but I just can't see, speak, or feel much beyond a general warmth. If I had died it seems like I would be seeing something happening. Like angels dancing around me in skimpy outfits. I can't say how long I've been like this. I think only a couple of hours. I try to remember what happened. I remember going to that party at that new club and dancing with that girl with the anchor tattooed on the back of her neck. I remember drinking champagne, wine, and bourbon and buying bottles for the ever-expanding group at my table. Who *were* those people anyway? I don't usually throw my money at just anyone, but I must have been feeling generous. From there it gets fuzzy. I do remember leaving the club...and I remember arguing with the valet to get my car...oh, Jesus, did I drive? I can't remember getting in the car. My memory of that night ends there. This is not good.

Still in absolute darkness with limited senses I try to catch more of what Mr. Whistle says, but he usually steps too far away for me to hear. I call him Mr. Whistle because his "s" comes out in a faint whistle. It reminds me of the beaver in the Disney movie *Lady and the Tramp*. Now I'm wondering how the hell I remember *Lady and the Tramp*, as I haven't seen it any time recently. Perhaps it's just the naughty title that keeps it in mind. But back to Mr. Whistle. I can tell he's a doctor. He gives orders to others in medical speak, most of which I don't understand. Then there's Kathleen Turner. I guess she's a nurse. She seems to be by my side a lot, but only for short time periods. Her voice is deep and just on the edge of masculine, but incredibly sexy. She sounds like the actress Kathleen Turner, so that is what I name her since I do not know her real name. I sense her leaning close to me, sense her touching me, but I never feel her hands. I know I'm in a hospital because of the occasional announcements I hear over the PA system in the distance and the squeaks of shoes on a linoleum floor as people move around. Then there are my parents, the only familiar voices that hover around me. I spent my whole life trying to pull away from those voices, and now I feverishly hang on to each word they utter, as if they will tumble into my mouth and allow me to speak. I feel better when I hear my parents talking to me. That sound tells me that I'm alive and that something is being done to help me. I feel overwhelmed when all the voices leave me and I'm all alone in the dark and quiet. I'll admit that this enveloping warmth is not all it's cracked up to be. I want to move. I want to see. I want to speak. I'm paralyzed. Oh, God, am I paralyzed? I try to bring my hands up to my face. I can't even feel my hands, or my face. Don't panic. Go back to the timeline. The timeline keeps me calm. Senior year at Stanford. Yes, that's a good memory. And just as I am reliving my time in the apartment I shared with two roommates and the party we threw that involved two arrests, three strippers, and the song "Just a Girl" on repeat, I hear a voice close to me.

"Hi, Cole, how are you doing today?" It's Kathleen Turner. I am instantly pulled off my timeline and struggle to find the source of her voice in the gloom. But all is quiet except for the occasional clink of metal and a machine beeping. *Please say something again.* It feels as if the words are coming out of my mouth. Something troubles me about the way Kathleen Turner's words do not pose a question to me. It is more of a statement, a matter of fact. As if she does not expect an answer.

"It's pourin' rain out there today. You know, the kind of rain where only four drops can soak you. And I forgot my umbrella, *and* I had to park in the far lot today." She sighs and I long to feel her breath on my cheek. I long to feel something. "Your parents are coming today," she says with a cheerful note.

Good. Maybe they will tell me what is happening. I feel silly, like a little boy asking for his parents. But in this sea of never-ending darkness on which I float, they are a small island upon which I can crawl.

"Do you know that your father actually winked at me and called me 'honey' the last time he was here? I couldn't believe it! I was sure your mother saw, but she never said anything. Boy, I'd best stay away from your father; he's trouble isn't he?" But Kathleen Turner chuckles softly through her indignation.

Yep, that's my father all right. Still a chauvinist, even in his sixties. And that sounds just like Mom, ignoring him and acting like he isn't a colossal jerk. I hear the rustling of crisp sheets. I try to will my eyelids to open, but I can't feel them. I can't tell where they are, and I can't find the muscle that controls them. I have tried this before. I can hear Kathleen Turner's shoes slide across the floor as she moves around to my left. Then I hear a soft crinkle of paper and perhaps the sound of paper sliding through hands.

"Still the same," Kathleen Turner sighs. "Still the same," she mutters. "I'll see you tomorrow, Cole." Her voice trails away even as she says it.

No! Wait! Please come back! I need more information. Is this a coma? Do you know I am conscious? Do you know I can hear you? Do you think I'm going to die? Because I'm not! I'm still here!

Dammit.

This is like that nightmare when you try to scream but you can't. Only I have no idea how long this nightmare has been going on.

3 THE WEIGHT OF TRUTH

One thing I am beginning to understand is that my concept of time has disappeared. I can't tell a minute from an hour, an hour from a day. At times I think that I must have just woken up from a sleep because I can feel that heavy veil of grogginess on my mind that you feel when you first wake up. But sleep blends into wakefulness when you are always in the dark. I don't know how long I sleep and my dreams confuse me into thinking that everything is back to normal. When I get the urge to yawn, my mouth doesn't move. It's maddening and frustrating like nothing I've ever experienced before.

My sense of hearing is all I can rely on, and never before have I listened so hard for sounds, any sounds. Sometimes I can hear soft voices coming from what I assume is a nurse's station. I often hear the faint ringing of a phone, papers being shuffled, and occasional laughter and conversation. I believe that this is when the door to my room is open. When everything else is quiet, I cling to these sounds as a sign that my situation hasn't changed. It's when there is total silence that I start to wonder if something has changed, if I have gone somewhere else. Yes, the possibility that I might die has crossed my mind. I understand the peril of being in a comatose state, and have heard the serious undertone in the doctor's and nurse's voices when they speak about me. I realize that I might just slip away at any moment and go wherever I'm supposed to go. I don't mind saying that the thought of that scares the hell out of me, especially if I stay in this darkness. I don't pretend to know what happens when we die; I only know what I hope happens. And I hope being able to see—*something, anything*—is part of it. So when it is completely quiet all around me, I begin to wonder if I have slipped off my life raft in this ocean of darkness and am sinking down to the sea floor. I strain my ears for a voice, a squeaky wheel on a gurney, or soft tennis shoe footsteps on the linoleum floor. Even the infrequent beep of the machine close to me brings relief. But when the silence presses in, its nothingness becoming almost an oxymoronic roar of white noise, and I struggle not to panic and lose my mind. The mind begins to play tricks on you when you are locked in darkness and silence. There is absolutely no context to existence. I try to focus on my life and revisit past events in order to calm myself.

My mind goes to the office. I think about my colleagues and my corner office on the sixty-fifth floor with its two walls of floor-to-ceiling windows. I think about the Sherman Industries acquisition and all that needs to be done. I think of the thousands of e-mails and voice mails that are filling my inbox. But then another thought hits me: What if I have been in the hospital so long that someone else has taken over my job? Could Stevens be sitting in my ergonomic leather model #SL46 chair right now? Goddamn Stevens. He was my competition for CFO and was served quite the ego blow when I got it. I'm sure he would gleefully fill in for me in my absence. I picture a cartoonish shake of a closed fist. What about the board of directors? Why haven't they been in to see me? Or have they come in, and I just can't remember? I can think of at least ten people from the office who I would expect to come visit me in the hospital. At least, I think they would. I try not to feel indignant since I can't vouch for my memory in this state. Each question seems to lead to another. What injury put me in a coma in the first place? Is my head bashed in? Is my face a mess? My brain must be relatively OK. I mean, I'm thinking rationally, aren't I? I need a doctor in here so I can get some clues about my condition. It seems like a long time since a doctor has been in here, which makes me think that I've been in a coma longer than I would like to believe. Common sense tells me that had I been a new case or my condition was worsening, or getting better for that matter, I would hear more urgent doctor-speak instead of merely relaxed, routine nurse-speak. This thought frightens me and I choose to think about my last vacation in Costa Rica instead. But the noise of a doorknob turning interrupts my thoughts and feels like a ray of light shining through an open door into my dark room. I hear footsteps and it sounds like more than two people. I hear what sounds like a coat and bag being set on something over to my right. Then there is the sound of something solid and ceramic being set on wood. The footsteps come closer.

"Hi, Cole. Hi, sweetie," my mother says softly. God, how I wish to open my eyes and respond to her. I can sense her very near to me, perhaps leaning over me, but I cannot feel a touch or that dip in the mattress you feel when someone sits down on your bed. "We brought you some irises, Cole. I didn't know if you liked flowers, but...well, they are my favorite, and I thought they would look nice in here." Her voice trails off, but I sense it is not because she moves away from me. I hear the ceramic sound on the wood again, and my father speaks in his gruff voice tinged with a southern accent.

"Don't put 'em there, Nancy, they'll be in the way of the nurses. They'll knock them over," he says. My father is always bossing my mother around. And always criticizing.

"Well, I want him to be able to smell them. The nurses said that he might be able to smell," my mother says quietly. I hear hope in her voice.

"That's a load of bull. He can't smell nothin'," my sensitive father proclaims. But then I start to wonder— can I smell anything? I hadn't noticed that I could. I inhale deeply, or at least I think I do, though I don't feel my chest rise.

"I want them here next to him, in case there is a chance he can smell," my mother insists.

"Put 'em on the window sill so they can get some goddamn sun. Why do you think flowers die so quickly in hospitals? All the medicines and sickness and fluorescent light kills 'em off." I hear my father plop down in a chair.

"John, for God's sake, can't you speak more positively around Cole?" my mother pleads.

"Why, 'cause he can hear as well as he can smell? He can't hear a goddamned thing," he mumbles.

"John!" my mother hisses. I hear paper rustling near me. I think from the dry, crispy-thin sound of it that it's a newspaper. "Now, Cole," she says with a note of determination, "I brought the business pages for you today. There are some interesting headlines this week." Her voice is upbeat, yet I can hear a strained note in it. I recognize that note of strain from when I do something she doesn't approve of, and she is faking optimism. It never felt good then, and it doesn't feel good now. But when my mother begins to read the articles aloud to me, I feel a sense of intense relief at hearing someone continuously talk to me. I cling to every word, not for the story it tells but to hear the inflection in her voice, the tone, and the way she starts each new sentence on a slightly higher note. These are things I have never noticed before about the way people speak. The way you can hear when they swallow, how they breathe through their sentences, how they pause, or how they click their tongues on a certain vowel as it slips from their mouths. I don't know how long my mother has been reading to me, but I don't think any amount of time could be long enough. I try to ignore the not-so-subtle sighs my father frequently emits, which sound crushingly like boredom laced with sarcasm. At one time, I would have read each and every one of those articles. I would have been focused and serious, taking mental notes for my future business deals. I would have cared which firm formed a joint venture with which, whose CFO was caught embezzling money, and whose marketing strategy for a new product made it sell like gangbusters in the thirteen- to seventeen-year-old demographic segment. But now they are just words that play out like a long song. And I have the feeling that Mother knows I don't really care about the headlines. I have the feeling that she *knows* that I am listening to her voice. The sound of the doorknob turning cuts through my mother's voice. I hear the newspaper being set down quickly.

"Mr. and Mrs. Suter, how are you today?" Kathleen Turner asks from the foot of my bed.

"Well, we are just fine, thank you. I was just reading Cole the paper since you said, well you said that maybe…" My mother is interrupted by my father clearing his throat loudly. I hear the leather on his chair protest and his feet scrape softly against the floor as he stands up.

"Anything new nurse?" my father asks loudly. But I still hear my mother sigh.

"I'm afraid not. His vitals are the same and so is his level of brain activity. But as we keep saying, that level of brain activity is definitely a hope to hold on to. Something is going on in there, but he just hasn't been able to push through the fog yet." Her voice gets closer as she approaches and then makes noises with something plastic sounding to my left. Then something happens for which I am completely unprepared. My left eye opens, and I'm assaulted by bright light. My instinct is to squint my eye against the harsh light, but I cannot move a muscle, and just when I think I glimpse an image in front of the blinding light—my eye closes again. My mind races to process what just happened, and I realize that Kathleen Turner had opened my eyelid, peered at my eye for a moment, and then closed it again. Although the initial shock of it surprises me, I now wish for it again so that I can again experience the precious gift of sight—if only for a moment.

"Did it dilate?" my mother asks hopefully.

"No. Still nonresponsive," Kathleen Turner answers. My mother says nothing and I try to picture her face.

"Mr. and Mrs. Suter, in cases of severe head trauma, such as Cole's, a comatose state typically lasts one to two weeks. As Dr. Benton told you, after this point in time the patient usually comes out of the comatose state, or..." She trails off. I hear my mother sniff and her next words are slightly choked by tears.

"Yes, yes, but it's only been two and a half weeks, so there is real hope that he will still come out of it, right?" my mother asks with desperation. "Cole is strong. He is strong! I know he's fighting this." Her last word ends in a sob.

"Of course, there is still that possibility. And there is

certainly nothing wrong with hope." I can almost feel Kathleen Turner smile at my parents. My father speaks next.

"Yeah, but what's he gonna wake up *to*?" he asks incredulously.

"That's enough, John," Mother says flatly.

"I mean just look at him!" His words chill me.

"John, I said that is *enough*," Mother spits the words this time. There are a few moments of silence. When he speaks again, it's softer and without aggression.

"Well, what if he never wakes up, nurse? What if he just stays like this?"

"It's very rare for patients to remain in a comatose state for extended periods of time. Hollywood likes to play with this medical phenomenon quite a bit, however those movies are largely exaggerated," she says gently. I hear the soft pad of tennis shoes on the floor, heading away from me. Kathleen Turner's voice is soft and kind and further away when she speaks again. "If Cole is anything like you have described him, he could very well push through this. He sounds like a strong-willed person. Don't give up hope." she finishes. The tennis shoes squeak and pad away and I hear the door opening and closing again with a soft click. I listen to my mother cry and wait to hear my father comfort her. I can only hope that they are embracing. However, knowing my father, they are not.

4 PUSH

After my parents leave, I think hard about everything I just heard. So, I have been like this for two and a half weeks—that isn't so bad, right? And I might not die, but probably will, according to Kathleen Turner. But what does she know? She follows rugged men around the Middle East in pursuit of gemstones. Or at least she did in *Jewel of the Nile*. I think that since my mind seems to still be in working order that surely I can make myself better. I can force myself awake. I've been hearing about the power of positive thinking for years. Maybe it is time to try it out. If I could sigh and roll my eyes right now, I would. Positive thinking. Positive...thinking. OK, I can do this. I try to remember what one of my girlfriends told me about focusing on the light and envisioning something. Ana was her name. She lasted about a month. She was too bohemian for me. But she might have been on to something with the focused positive thinking...if only I had listened. I think she told me to envision what I wanted. At the time I remember thinking I wanted *her*, in my bed, naked. Oh, but what was the thing about the auras of light, or the colors or something? Pick a color and see it in the air? *Fuck.* I don't know. My listening skills, especially with Ana, were apparently very weak. And I know I'm like that with most women, if not all. I don't know when exactly I became "that guy." You know the one. The guy who sees sex as a challenge, a conquest, and spares no feelings between hello and good-bye. That's me; I'm that guy. A small part of me feels a little guilt at what my mother would think if she knew how I had treated most of the women in my life.

"Envision what you want," Ana had told me. I want out of this bed. I want out of this darkness. I picture myself opening my eyes and seeing the room around me. I picture a potted flowering plant close to my bed where my mother set it. I see ugly hospital visitor chairs to my right. I see the nurse's station out the door. I see beautiful nurses with short skirts and fishnet stockings. No, wait. Don't get side tracked! I picture sitting up in bed, seeing white sheets and blankets fall away from my chest and into my lap. I swing my legs over to the side of the bed and hop down. I try hard to feel the cool linoleum on my bare feet. I *think* it, but I'm not sure I can *feel* it. And still, there's only darkness. I need to find a way to push through the black wall in front of me. If only my parents could have someone come in to coach me through this, if only they knew that I am listening, then maybe an expert psychologist would know how to talk me through it and help me take each brick down from the wall until I could walk through.

One phrase keeps repeating itself in my mind: "severe head trauma." I have finally discovered the reason I am in the coma. And this fact makes me worry even more about whether I can come out of this. If my brain is on vacation, it may never want to go back to the real world of pain and swelling and…damage. Sure, I can *think* clearly, but what if when I wake up I find that

I have lost my language skills, my motor skills, or other basic skills? They could be gone and I just don't know it yet. The prospect is almost too frightening to bear. I picture myself in a wheelchair for the rest of my life, living with my parents, being dressed and fed by my mother while my father looks on in disgust. I may never walk again. I may never talk again. I may never have sex again. I may live with my parents again.

Jesus, God, Lord of mercy, please help me push out of this and be OK.

Ah, suddenly I'm a religious man. Never have been before, but this seems like the prime time to start talking to God. Forget the positive thinking; let's go straight to the big guy in the sky. But will God know I'm a fraud? Probably, considering I haven't spoken to God since I was about thirteen and prayed that I would pitch a no-hitter in the championship game, and when that didn't happen I started to question where God was. I didn't lose my faith because someone close to me had died or because I saw the suffering of hundreds of people on TV. No, I lost it when God failed to help me pitch a no-hitter. Granted, my parents never really did instill religious teachings in me. In fact, the first time I saw a family say grace before dinner was at a friend's house when I was seven years old. I watched their bowed heads as they said a lovely thanks over a meat loaf. I remember thinking that it was weird, but also strangely comforting. But now I doubt that God has forgotten that I lost faith over a baseball game and will be willing to let me just jump back on the bandwagon in my time of crisis. And I doubt I'm in good standing, what with the way I have lived my life the last several, OK, ten years. But just in case God *is* listening, and maybe *is* forgetful, I pray. I reach down into the depths of my mind or my soul and form a prayer. It comes out in fragments. Sentences that don't really make sense rush together, but somehow I can't stop the flow. I start the prayer with shyness, hesitation, and embarrassment. I move into a serious and near-pleading tone as the words come faster and faster. By the end I can feel emotion welling up and flooding me, and my voice is the voice of pure desperation inside my head, uttering a plea so tangible that I can almost taste it in my mouth.

5 OCEAN FLOOR

When I was eight, I almost drowned in the neighbor's pool. I was roughhousing with the other boys my age, and we were throwing a football around, playing keep-away. One of the boy's elbows came down hard on my temple, and I was momentarily knocked out. I slipped under the water and began to sink. At first no one noticed in the commotion of yelling boys and laughter. I was drifting slowly toward the bottom of the deep end, motionless. When I regained consciousness underneath the water, I opened my eyes and saw the rough concrete bottom of the pool near my face and the white plastic drain a few feet away. A stab of panic pierced me. Then I felt arms around my torso and my body was lifted up and up and up for what felt like forever as my lungs burned. We broke the surface and starbursts obstructed my vision as my brain screamed for oxygen. I never suffered any ill effects from that day, but I find myself thinking about it now. This perpetual darkness, void of physical feeling, has me imagining I am floating in water, my body entirely motionless. My brain must be serving that memory up as a premonition, because a few minutes later, I experience something similar to that day in the pool.

It must be nighttime because the hum of the hospital has quieted, and I only hear the occasional padding of tennis shoes on the floor outside the room. I long for the din of daytime, for the interesting noises the hospital presents. This night is especially quiet. It is in this quiet, in this dark and floating state, that I hear the most disturbing noise I've ever heard. It's the vital sign alarm monitor sounding. For a split second, the sound of the different beeps confuses me, then dread sets in. Something is going wrong in my body. This time, instead of the padding of shoes on linoleum, I hear squeaks as feet rush toward me. I hear wheels move quickly on the floor, and aluminum equipment banging together. I sense the presence of several people all at once. I'm overwhelmed with sensation after being in the void for so long. I can hardly focus on any one sound.

"Heart rate forty-one. BP dropping," a male voice on my right says matter-of-factly. There is more bustling around and more voices. I try to focus but can't, and all the voices begin to meld together. I feel as if I'm spinning and can't grab onto anything solid. I hear a second, different alarm go off in the room. There are more voices now, some yelling.

The voices and noises start to fade into the background and I feel a strange sensation. Something is pulling me gently, though I can't say in which direction. I don't feel that I'm going up, down, or sideways, just pulling away from my surroundings. I drift away and a vision appears. It is the first thing I've seen in a while, yet the light does not hurt my eyes, and I feel no surprise at regaining my vision. I am floating on the surface of a calm sea. As far as I am able to see it's just water, and more water. The water laps lazily at my chin and cheeks. I start to slip slowly under the surface, though not in a natural way. I'm aware that I am not in control of my body. A few last little waves lap at my forehead, and then I submerge. I am floating toward the bottom of, not a pool, but a vast ocean. The ocean is crystal clear and I can see the smooth sandy bottom far below. I'm not scared and I don't feel a need to panic anymore. I just calmly watch the sunlight filtering through the sea to the sand as the sea floor comes closer. I don't worry. I don't move. I don't care. It is OK. I think I just died. But it's OK. I don't know why, but it's OK.

I sink deeper and come closer to the bottom and now I can see the hard ripples formed in the sand by the constant ocean current. Not a creature or plant is in sight. Bare sand and sparkling water surround me. As I come within feet of the bottom I brace myself for the landing, out of instinct I think, although I still feel that there is nothing to worry about. But when I reach the sand I feel not a hard bump, but a slippery sensation, and I keep falling downward. I move down through the sand, and as I sink lower, I see it enveloping my face, shifting and pouring around me. As I fall out of the sand floor my mind reels as I try to figure out which way is up and whether I'm still falling. I briefly glimpse a purplish light and then I'm suddenly tugged with such force that my stomach feels like it has been left behind. Instantly I am speeding through water, being pulled in random directions, faster and faster until my vision is blurred. I have no control and picture my limbs dragging behind me like those of a rag doll. A whooshing sound fills my ears and the force tugs me until I no longer can see anything. An intense orange glow fills my vision. It's so bright and vivid that I squint my eyes and feel the rush of air around me. There's pressure and more light and then…silence. Complete and utter silence and stillness. I have stopped.

Everything has stopped. It is as if someone has turned off the music, going instantly from a volume of fifty to zero. I open my eyes.

6 HEAVEN

My brain immediately recognizes sunlight, but I do not feel the need to squint. The next thing I see is a large brown horse standing directly in front of me. Needless to say I'm not prepared for that. The horse is so big that its head towers over me and I can see up its enormous nostrils. I have never seen a horse so big and intimidating. If this is heaven, is this a chariot of sorts? The horse exhales loudly into my face and stamps a hoof, and I take a step backward. Or at least, it seems like I did, but I don't feel my body move. I try to look down at my legs, but I find that I cannot move my head. I feel the same as I did lying in the hospital bed except that now I am standing upright, somewhere in a sunlit field with a freakin' Clydesdale. Thoroughly confused, I will myself not to panic since it seems that I just died, and wherever I am now has to be better than being imprisoned in the dark while stuck in a hospital bed.

Suddenly, an adult female voice behind me says, "Oh for Heaven's sake, Jenny—he won't hurt you!" The voice stimulates my brain into working my legs because I turn around to face it. A middle-aged woman stands near me, her thick red hair secured in a low ponytail under her cowboy hat. She is very tall, unusually so, just like the horse. I'm six feet tall; I have never felt so short since I was a little kid. I don't recognize this woman, nor do I recognize the landscape around me, I realize, now that I can see more of it. I am standing in a small fenced ring of bare dirt with a wood post in the ground to which reins tie the brown horse. Beyond the fence, lush green grass stretches out over lazy rolling hills dotted with trees as far as I can see. A modest barn stands close by, its red paint peeling and faded, its double doors open to the warm sunshine. It is not at all what I had pictured heaven would look like, but I decide it's fine with me, and I actually feel a calmness wash over me. That is until I hear my response to the woman. And in the back of my mind I am still trying to make sense of the fact that she has just called me Jenny.

"I just don't want to yet," I mumble quietly. Only it isn't me who speaks. It is the voice of a young girl and it surrounds my head like headphones would sound. Trepidation creeps over me. Something isn't right. I look down at my legs—only I haven't willed myself to do it. I realize with dread that I am not really *looking* at things, I am being *shown* my surroundings, as if I am watching a movie, with no control over where the camera will pan next. When I see my legs the dread settles in. These are not my legs. They are short and skinny and clad in faded pink corduroy pants. The shoes peeking out from the cuffs of the pants are small brown cowboy boots—a child's boots. I want to panic.

"Jenny, we've been standing out here for fifteen minutes while you've been decidin' whether or not to ride that horse. Now you can hop up there right quick and see what a fuss you've been makin' over nothin', or you can forget it and we will go on and get supper started early. It's your choice," the older woman says impatiently.

I try to open my mouth to speak, but I am as incapable of that as I was when I was lying on that hospital bed. Instead, my view of the ground moves up and I see my hand reach out hesitantly toward the giant horse. My petite child's hand. Inside I am hyperventilating, but outside nothing is happening to reflect that. I am a bundle of emotions trapped in a locked box. *Whose body am I in?* I watch as the hand extends from the child's body and softly touches the horse's neck. I wait for sensation. I wait for the feel of horse hair on my fingertips. But I feel nothing as the hand moves slowly up the neck of the horse and gently combs through the horse's mane. It reminds me of that sick feeling when you wake up in the middle of the night and your entire arm is numb because you have been laying on it, cutting off the circulation. You rub that arm but it's completely numb to the touch. My brain says I should feel the horse, but the hand I see is betraying that truth. The voice echoes in my head again.

"I want to ride…but I'm scared," says the girl's voice. It is soft and very young.

"Well, scared never got anyone anywhere, did it?" the older woman says sharply. She is starting to remind me of my father. "C'mon now. Just like we practiced on the saddle. Grab the horn with your left hand, there you go." My vantage point shifts and I am now next to the horse. I watch as the little hand reaches up and grasps the saddle horn, which seems impossibly high up. My view goes down to see the little brown cowboy boot slide slowly into the stirrup. The horse stamps a back foot impatiently in the dust, and in that moment the most intense feeling of anxiety washes over me. I feel it like a hot shower burning my face. It's a thick feeling of dread and fear, and although I don't know what is causing it, it seems to be my own emotion. I feel it *in* me, kicking my brain into flight or fight response. If I could have felt my heart beating I'm sure it would have been pounding against my ribs. But I still can't feel a thing, and it's extremely unnerving.

"One…two…three—up you go!" the woman says. My view rises up over the horses back and I am able to see just over the top of the saddle, but suddenly I shoot back down to the ground and am beside the horse again. The fear I feel is so great that it almost seems like I can taste it. My view is now just the small legs and feet, the small hands grasped together, twisting in anxiety.

"Now c'mon, Jenny, you were almost there! Why'd you stop?"

"I'm, I'm…I can't," the girl stammers and backs away from the horse. Then something happens that serves to confuse and enlighten me all at once. My vision blurs like the surface of a slightly disturbed pond: wavy and rippled. It's something every human knows well: tears. Tears that blur the vision while catching the bright sunlight. I hear her sniffle and emit a choked word or two in the way a child does when crying. I am seeing this young girl's tears. I am seeing them…through her eyes. My vision is her vision. I cannot begin to comprehend this and my frenzied mind tries to make sense of it. I suddenly picture myself sitting cross-legged inside someone's head. It's a bizarre image but my mind took me there so I go with it. I am sitting in someone's head and looking out through two portholes into the world. The holes are this girl's line of sight. I have no control over what I am seeing because it is determined by where she looks. And then it hits me that the extreme anxiety and fear I had felt so intensely came from her. It is *her* anxiety and fear. It's the only thing that makes sense to me. And I'm looking for anything that makes sense at this point. I'm not scared of horses, I don't have fear or anxiety around them, and

I'm quite sure that the emotions I feel are not related to my worry about heaven or whatever it is that is happening to me. Those emotions are not my own.

"Alright, then. Let's take Stormy on in for the night, and then we'll go start supper," the woman says, more softly. A sense of relief washes through me without warning, as the girl is given permission to stop trying.

Walking feels like a whole new experience. I feel almost dizzy as the world bounces slightly up and down. I want to hang onto something to steady myself. But there is nothing to hang onto, and all I can do is watch helplessly as the girl drops her head to stare at her feet and my view of the ground ahead of me changes. I feel slightly nauseated, and my mind aches for control of my legs and my eyes. It's like sitting on someone's shoulders as they walk. You feel out of control as someone else's legs are doing the walking, and all you can do is hold onto the shoulders. This is how it feels, and honestly, I want *down*.

The girl, Jenny, takes me along for the ride as she and the woman lead the horse into the barn, remove the saddle, and curry comb the horse. Being in Jenny reminds me of what it feels like to be small, and my mind struggles to readjust to the new perspective. As she walks toward a white clapboard house across a small field, the dizzy bouncing feeling returns and I struggle once more to get used to this way of "hitching a ride." I hadn't noticed the house before since the girl had not looked that way. I am completely bound by the limitations of the body I seem to be in. I only see what she wants to look at. As she nears the house, she turns and looks at two trucks in the driveway. I spot a white cat sitting on the rim of the truck bed and realize that is what she is looking at when she makes a soft cooing noise and the cat pricks up its ears. I can also see the license plate on the truck and just make out the state before Jenny looks back toward the house: Missouri. I am in Missouri? Missouri is heaven? Nope. Impossible. Plus, logic tells me I am not in heaven but trapped somewhere else. The thought of reincarnation occurs to me, and while I don't believe in this, it's the only explanation that comes to mind. Could it be? But, if I had been reincarnated, wouldn't I be this person and be able to control this body. There is no more time to ponder this question because Jenny reaches the house and opens the door to walk in, and now there are a myriad of things to take in.

The house is a farmhouse, and Jenny has entered through a side door into a spacious kitchen. At the large, round dining table in the middle of the floor, a tall, lean man sits reading the newspaper. He looks up and smiles at me. Or her. His smile is so kind that I instinctively smile back, but I suppose he can't see that because that happens only in my mind. Is she smiling? I think so because I feel good feelings around me as soon as she sees him.

"How did you and Stormy do, Jenny?" He has a deep and gravelly voice that doesn't seem to match his lean frame. But then I see the pack of cigarettes on the table in front of him and think it might account for the roughness.

"I didn't get on her, Dad," Jenny says shamefacedly, looking down at the table where she is picking at the wood.

"That's all right honey. It just takes some getting used to. You'll ride her when you and Stormy are both ready. Maybe next time huh?" His kind words make her look up at him and this time I can feel her smile. It's a sensation so positive that it seems to brighten the room around us. I hear the door open and shut behind me and assume the woman has entered. I hear water running and the metallic splashing sound it makes as it fills a large pot. Over this noise the woman begins barking orders at the girl for supper preparations. Her dad winks at her as she turns to gather plates from the cabinet.

"Laura, we're out of napkins," I hear the girl say. At first I'm not sure to whom she is speaking, but then the woman turns from the sink to answer.

"The new pack is in the pantry." I guess from the girl's address that the woman is not Jenny's mother. Perhaps she's a stepmother. I try to take in as much of the surroundings as possible as Jenny moves around the kitchen. Watching the movie of Jenny's life, waiting to see what the camera will show me next, I take in the thin and faded curtains hanging limply at the windows. The pale yellow linoleum floor is pockmarked from years of dropped items, scuffed from chair legs, and bears the occasional stain. A wooden sign hanging above the door asks someone to "Bless this house." With a sarcasm that comes naturally to me, I realize I am in the heartland, the Bible belt, the antithesis of my life. I begin to look at the run-down house with disgust, judging it even as I realize I'm being unfair. But I can't stop. When Jenny turns around to grab the salt and pepper shakers from the counter I see a small wooden cross hanging on the wall. I can feel myself smirking. If they only knew that God and religion are nowhere close to being involved in death. I know what they don't— there is no God. If there was a God I wouldn't be stuck in this girl's body, doomed to watch her life forever.

"All right now, supper's ready. Jenny did you wash your hands?" The woman sighs and wipes her hands on her dirty apron. Her face is pinched and speaks of unhappiness. Her eyes hold an anger that I don't yet understand. She sits down stiffly at the table and clasps her hands in front of her, looking irritated. Another shitty marriage, I think. Another couple stuck in the confines of the societal norm with no end in sight. Jenny whirls around to the sink, making me dizzy. I watch as she scrubs her hands with the bar of soap lying to the side. Another emotion: apprehension. I'm not sure why I would feel this way, so I have to believe that it isn't me that is apprehensive, but Jenny. When she turns around and rushes to her seat at the table, I see Laura looking at her with a frown on her face, while her father beams kindly at her. The dichotomy is striking.

Throughout the meal I begin to think that perhaps the tension comes from something other than an unhappy marriage. The man and the woman don't speak unkindly to each other. But the woman is very hard on Jenny, and while her father seems to be a kind man with great affection for his daughter, he does not stand up for her when the woman is being unfair. I feel the swirl of emotions shift from apprehension to deep sadness. I can't see the man and woman very much during the dinner since Jenny looks down at her plate so much of the time. But when her father speaks to her she holds his gaze and I feel her tension ease.

"I'm really proud of how your grades are looking Jenny," he says, while shaking half the salt container onto his mashed potatoes. "Especially English and Science. Keep it up," he winks at her across the table. I can feel the tension drain away as she locks onto his eyes as if they are a lifeline. But the line is broken when she meets Laura's cold eyes looking down at her. Jenny looks at her plate again and begins to make designs in her mashed potatoes.

~

The evening grows darker, and I still have not seen the rest of the house because Jenny mostly stays in the modest living room with its faded paintings of barns and covered bridges adorning the walls. She sits on the couch, cutting paper strips into loops, and linking them together one by one with tape. She does this for what seems like hours. But because I am feeling very content and calm, I don't really mind. I am enveloped by a soothing feeling and yet also an almost frenzied urge to push on and not let the calm slip away. As I watch her little hands carefully cut the red paper into strips and then tape them around each other repeatedly, I feel like she *needs* to do this task in order to feel calm. Obsessive compulsive, I wonder? Or maybe just a form of escape from whatever it is that bothers her. The paper chains drape across the couch, trail onto the floor, and wind around the living room. When Laura calls to her from the other room and says it's time for bed Jenny stiffens and stops what she's doing. Her eyes trace the length of the chain all the way to the end. I hear her sigh and almost feel her mentally climbing the chain to escape to somewhere else.

~

The night is lonely. This is the most alone I have ever felt. Even when I was lying in the hospital bed unable to move or speak I didn't feel this alone. I feel utterly trapped. Being in a body that *can* move, speak and feel, yet having no control over when it can do so is more frustrating. I hear the girl softly snoring, the breeze ruffling the curtains at the window, and the incessant screaming of locusts outside. Everything is dark. While Jenny's eyes are closed, I have lost my sight too. Now I'm bored. I don't think too much about why I can't sleep along with her. I don't feel the biological need to sleep, so the night is interminable. Several times I try to will her awake. I try yelling "Wake up!" even though I know by now I can't bring the words to life and she couldn't hear them anyway. Next I attempt to share my emotions with her, as she seems to do with me. I try to send her a feeling of alarm, hoping to rouse her from her deep sleep. I focus on a warning, on alertness, even the sound of a siren. But she sleeps on, unaware of my presence. If this is what my eternity is, I think I would have taken the fire and brimstone of hell just to have something more interesting to see. But if I don't believe in God, then I don't believe in hell, right? I don't know anymore.

~

Around seven in the morning the world returns as Jenny opens her eyes. I have a bit of warning as she stirs in the bed, and I sense and hear the movement so I am prepared for the onslaught of light. I see that the sheets are tangled tightly around her legs and am not surprised since I had heard her tossing and turning throughout the night. It is the strangest thing, to sense and hear that this body is moving, but not to feel it around you actually moving. And I notice that I don't feel dizzy when she is moving around in the bed. But when her eyes open and she hops out of bed I feel as if the floor tilts. It seems that looking through someone else's eyes while not being in control of their body causes the sensation for me.

I feel alert and ready to look at new things as Jenny slowly moves about her small room. When she opens her closet door, I see more of the paper chains hanging next to clothes hung from the wooden rod. Both ends of the multiple chains hang to the floor and tickle the hard wood as they sway in the breeze generated by the opening of the door. She changes into her clothes for the day and is walking toward her bedroom door when she stops abruptly. She cocks her head and I listen as well. Faint voices come from somewhere down the hall.

Jenny walks quietly to the door and cracks it open. I recognize the voices of her father and Laura, presumably coming from their bedroom.

"This isn't working," Laura says in a voice that sounds devoid of hope. They are getting a divorce I think smugly. I was right. I see Jenny's hand tighten on the doorframe, her knuckles whitening.

"We'll keep trying Laura. It will happen, we just have to keep trying and keep faith," Jenny's father replies, his voice soothing.

"I'm running out of faith, Bill. Why doesn't God grant me this? What have I done to deserve this?" Her voice rises in desperation.

"You know as well as I do that God does not punish. We all have trials; we just need to persist."

"We have *persisted* for three years, Bill," she spits out. "It's time to face reality."

"Well then reality might be adoption, Laura," he says this so softly that I am not sure I hear it. But when Jenny's hands both fall from the door frame to her sides in silent shock, I know I have heard correctly.

"I won't adopt! I won't. It's not the same and you know it. Plus we can't afford it."

"We could if we sold some horses," Bill says quietly. There is a long pause and I try to imagine the facial expressions that they both hold.

"No. I won't do that," she finally says firmly. I hear him sigh and the sound of footsteps pacing the wood floor.

"Then you need to come to terms with the fact that Jenny is your child for this lifetime. That's going to have to be enough for you. You have to face it, Laura. I know it's hard but I…"

Laura cuts him off. "It's harder than you know. And…it's not enough. She's…not enough." The words fall into the silence and hang in the humid morning air.

Painful knowledge and understanding hit Jenny, and I feel a well of sadness fill her more quickly than any emotion I have felt from her yet. It feels as if my heart is being dragged down into depression. I feel the overwhelming sadness that comes just before tears and know if I was fully aware I would have felt the sting in her eyes before the tears flow. Jenny shuts the door silently and returns to her bed, climbing under the covers even though she is fully dressed. I hear her crying and feel her pain as if it was my own. The intensity of the hurt surprises me, and I feel a deep longing for something which I can't identify.

After a while there is a knock at the door and her father comes in.

"Good morning, sleepy head!" he calls out cheerfully and sits on the edge of her bed.

"Hi," Jenny whispers. She meets his eyes and then looks away.

"Jenny, have you been crying?" He leans towards her and touches her shoulder to turn her towards him. She doesn't answer but instead reaches for a Kleenex on the nightstand and blows her nose. "What's wrong sweetie?"

"Nothing," she sniffs. "What time are we leaving?" She swings her legs off the bed. Her Dad doesn't answer right away so she looks up at him. His eyes are filled with concern and something else. Knowing. He clears his throat and looks away.

"We're leaving in ten," he says and pats her leg as he stands up and leaves the room. Again I feel the sadness coming from her. I can't stop it or block it in any way. This could really get to be a drag. She walks down the hallway to the bathroom and shuts the door. I try to read the words on a nearby shampoo bottle as she does her business and stares unblinking, because I feel uncomfortable and as if I'm invading her privacy. As she brushes her teeth she uses one of the little paper cups loaded in a dispenser on the tile wall next to the sink. For some reason that little detail screams "farm house" to me. You don't see that in bathrooms in the city. I keep waiting for her to look directly into the mirror above the sink so I can see what she looks like, but she never does. I find that odd. I myself love to look in the mirror. It's rewarding for me to see the results of my workouts in the flesh. But I guess six-pack abs don't matter to me anymore now. Jenny tosses her cup into the trash can and turns to the door. But then her gaze jerks back down to the trash can. She bends down and looks closer. Lying to the side on the inside of the basket is a pregnancy test stick. She picks it up slowly and stares at it for a long time. The blue words proclaim what she and I both already know. *Not pregnant.*

Her emotions wash over me. I feel...melancholy. That's the best way I can describe it. That feeling you get when something feels wrong with your day, but you are not sure what it is, you can't put your finger on it, but something is definitely off and...down. Except, I know what is wrong. I also detect feelings of rejection and resentment. I don't know how I can possibly know or feel these. But it's as distinct as if I am feeling it myself.

Am I?

How do I know these *aren't* my feelings and that I'm not somehow latching onto her life and connecting to it? But, why would I react to the events that just unfolded? I have no attachment to these people. Why would I care? I don't. Plus, I rarely feel rejection. Things always go my way. I make them go my way.

I never get to accompany Jenny to church. She struggles into a light blue summer dress that she grunts and pulls at in frustration when it doesn't fit right. She is walking down the hallway to the front door when she stops at a low table to pick up a stuffed dog. It is then that I glimpse the bottom edge of a mirror hanging on the wall above the table. But Jenny doesn't look up long enough for me to see anything but her waist and the stuffed dog in her hands. She stands silently for a moment, clutching the dog tightly and fingering the satin lining of its ears. Then, at the shrill burst of Laura's voice from outside calling to Jenny to hurry up, she turns and runs outside. As she throws open the front door something strange happens. A burst of orange light assaults me and I know instantly it isn't the sun. The world in front of me disappears and I hear the same whoosh of air I had heard when I left my hospital bed. The strange feeling of pressure returns and the air roars around me while the light permeates my brain. As I feel myself moving through the air and fighting against the tremendous pressure, one thought infiltrates the chaos: I never got to see Jenny's face.

7 BOOKS, LOVE AND DUST

Whirling through the light and dark I feel nauseated and dizzy. OK, I should be headed to where I need to go now, I think. I took a little detour and now I will be on the right road to the unearthly palace of souls. Just wait until I tell the others what happened. It could be my icebreaker in heaven. The first person I meet there will get to hear quite the story. *Hey, I'm Cole. Yep, yep, just arrived. Would I like a pair of angora slippers? Why, yes I would. A Patargus Series No. 4 cigar and a tumbler of Middleton? Don't mind if I do. And how did you end up here? Ahhh, wife killed you, huh? Well I can hardly blame her what with the way you've let yourself go. Me? Well I got on some kind of wrong astral plane and was inside a female brain for a while. Can't say I didn't occasionally wish for that during my life. Anyway, point me toward the bikini girls on the trampoline. If this is heaven, they must be here.*

But maybe the first "person" I will talk to will be God. How would *that* go? I'm not ready to think about that. I am ready to get there and get on with exploring a new world. Assuming that I don't just hit a black hole and disappear. If my soul is living right now, surely it

36

has some destination. But maybe it doesn't. That thought makes me a little nervous. I'm still spinning around in nothingness, but the spinning has slowed a bit. What happens next surprises me even more the second time. The dizzying whirl and roar abruptly end and a scene instantly appears before my eyes. *My* eyes?

I think I've taken another detour. Dammit. A huge bookshelf towers over me, filled to the edges with worn and faded book spines lined up like siding on an old barn. My hand reaches for a book two shelves above my head. Dammit, not *my* hand. I watch as a hand with hairy knuckles slowly pulls a two-inch-thick book carefully off the shelf. My knuckles definitely are not hairy. The book comes down in front of my eyes and I am able to read the title before the cover is gently pulled back by the hairy hands. *Cultural Anthropological Analysis of Brazil's Pua Tribe.* OK, now I know I must be in hell. Will I be forced to read this thing? Maybe the devil himself will come in and offer me slippers made of hot coals instead of angora and Wild Turkey in a Dixie cup. But the owner of the hands skims the table of contents quickly and closes the book with a soft thud of old paper. My view shifts as the man turns toward the aisle between bookshelves. Once again, I feel dizzy as he starts to walk. But it's even worse this time, because he seems to have a strange gait, pitching forward on the right foot. As we step out from the aisle, a whole library comes into view, so grand that I want to stare in wonder. All I catch are glimpses: a wide staircase descending between a vast, sky-lighted ceiling; modern lighting fixtures glowing down on framed artwork; and rows upon rows of flat screen monitors at computer stations. The man takes me not to the stairs but to an elevator off in the corner. As he walks into the old elevator and turns to face the front, I hear something softly thud on the floor. As soon as the ancient elevator doors come to a close with a shimmy and creak, the man starts mumbling to himself.

"Tuesday night...Sherry will be calling...around eight. Need to...ask her about the marathon and...how it went." The words are spoken softly and are accompanied by audible breaths forced out. I can't tell if he is nervous, or in pain, or if this is how he normally speaks, in halting phrases. The elevator groans to a stop, the doors open, and the man steps out into a modern section of the library. With each step he takes on the echoing linoleum floor I hear a tap and a slight scrape. A walking cane would account for this as well as the thud I heard when he got into the elevator, not to mention my dizzy ride. As we walk unsteadily to the counter, I try to take in as much information about my surroundings as I can. On this floor, new laptops are lined up in rows on tables in front of modern ergonomic chairs, and contemporary art is suspended from the ceiling by thin wires. As we near the counter, I see a woman standing and typing at a computer. When she looks up, her eyes crinkle at the edges as she smiles warmly at me. Or him, I suppose.

"Good afternoon! Long time no see," she says with a soft chuckle, and I hear the man laugh nervously. The woman looks to be in her fifties and is as thin as a rail. I hear my host speak again.

"Oh, yes. I was in...yesterday, wasn't I?" he says in his halting manner. His voice is low, soft, and nervous.

"Yes." The woman continues to smile at him. But it isn't the kind of smile that speaks of attraction, more the kind that is tinged with sympathy. "What an interesting book today. Very much out of your field isn't it?" she asks while she runs the book over a scanner.

"I, uh, yes, I suppose it is. Quite." I feel something strange coming over me. I feel a bit tense. A feeling of embarrassment hits me—the unmistakable feeling you get when you do something stupid and someone witnesses it. But the man hasn't done anything to embarrass himself as far as I can see.

"Well, nothing wrong with branching out, that's what I always say," she smiles again at him, and I detect a note of reassurance being beamed his way.

"Yes, uh, I tend to…think that also," he stammers. Embarrassment is joined by nervousness. And then it hits me. The man is shy. Painfully shy. I am experiencing his intense feelings of shyness. I've never been a shy person, far from it, so these feelings are new to me. Embarrassment isn't new, although I probably haven't felt it since high school. I just didn't know that being shy means feeling embarrassed. Or, at least it does for this guy.

"Have a nice day, Professor. I'll see you tomorrow then?" she says with a wink.

"What's that? Oh…yes, I believe…I believe you will…Margaret. Thank you." He turns and walks away. The poor guy can hardly converse. Maybe he has a thing for her? Whatever it is, I am not looking forward to experiencing his feelings again. Although, since he is a professor, maybe he is just odd. We make our dizzy way out the front door of the library and down a long ramp to the sidewalk. Tall buildings speak of academia; benches, flyer kiosks, and odd art sculptures dot the landscape. Young people hustle by holding backpacks, riding bikes. Some go by in twos, holding hands, others are reading textbooks while walking. It appears to be a bitterly cold day on this college campus. The cement sidewalk has that frozen appearance it gets when blowing snow swirls just a fraction of an inch above it. The snow finds its resting place on the grassy areas; sticking to the blades of grass, and the gray sky promises more. I don't see much of the campus because the man hunches over against the cold and mostly looks at the ground while walking. I watch the swirling snow form lazy patterns on the sidewalk. I don't feel much of anything from him now except maybe some slight anxiety. We walk for a while, and several passing students call out, "Hi Professor Trenholm!" Each time the man barely glances up but raises a hand slowly and greets each by name in his slow, deliberate voice, and sometimes by then the student is already long gone.

We enter a large brick building with "Letters, Arts, and Sciences" in gold metal lettering on the side and the kind of heavy double doors that make a racket when opening and closing. I wonder what part of the country I am in now. The weather at Jenny's house had been sunny and warm, and here it seems cold. And for that matter, is it the same day? Do I jump as instantly as it feels, or do I arrive days, weeks, or even months later? These questions bother me intensely, but I have no idea how to get the answers. The professor walks unsteadily down the echoing halls until he reaches a side hallway punctuated with dark wooden doors with inserts of frosted glass. He stops at the door whose etched glass reads "Professor Trenholm, PhD, English Literature." He unlocks the door and we enter a very small, very messy office. Bookshelves cover almost two full walls and a large desk takes up most of the floor. Or it could be that the desk is a normal size and the room is unbearably small. The man sets his book down on the desk with a deep sigh and walks over to the window across from the door. The glass looks old and wavy and gives the outside world a distorted shimmer. I enjoy the view out over the campus and the students walking quickly back and forth like colorful ants. His eyes look toward a thick bank of trees. When he doesn't shift his gaze, I get the impression it is an unseeing stare, the kind that happens when you are thinking so hard about something that your eyes nearly go out of focus, and you no longer see what is in front of you. For me to witness this feels odd. I don't know what thoughts hold him captive, so I feel uncomfortable, as if I am stuck in place. But soon he shifts away from the window with another sigh and sits down. I'm beginning to think this guy is either very dull or very depressed.

~

We seem to be there for hours as the professor reads through his students' essay papers. I am bored out of my mind (*my* mind?) after the first one and have no desire to go on reading them. I look at anything I can besides the writing—-the edges of the other papers on the desk, the professor's hands holding a pen and writing, and the pattern of his suit jacket that shows at the backs of his hands. His hands are wrinkled and dotted with age spots, so I put his age at around sixty-five or seventy. His nails are bitten and ragged, each and every one of them chewed down to the quick. As he reads on and writes notes to the students I long to go to sleep. Not that I'm tired, that's just what I would normally do in a situation like this. Will this guy ever take a break? Just when I have started to count the hairs on the dedicated professor's knuckles, there is a loud knock on the door. My view is instantly brought upward with the jerk of his head and I welcome the change of scenery. A shadowy figure of a man stands behind the frosted glass and I notice the professor's gaze seems riveted to the spot for a few seconds too long before he says, "Please." The door opens and a man in an ill-fitting suit enters. That is what I first notice—his suit. The man is obviously slender, and the suit is too big and bags shapelessly around his frame. I look closely for style indicators that would point to a designer, but determine it is most likely a department store special. I am disappointed. I love a great suit. The professor takes a sharp breath when the man enters: my window view of the world jerks ever so slightly at the same time I hear his breath.

"Hello, Alexander! I'm just stopping by to make sure you know about the budget meeting at four?" Ill-Fitting Suit Man asks with a slight cock of the head. His brown hair is wavy and slightly messy, and his thin and narrow face only exaggerates the size of his suit. The professor clears his throat, looks down at his desk, then up again quickly, making me dizzy.

"What's that? Why yes, I think…I…remember…" He trails off. The man at the door nods encouragingly and smiles warmly, as if he is speaking with a shy child. "I think I remember hearing about…that," my lame host finally finishes.

"Good! Miranda sent out the notice a bit last minute, so I just wanted to make sure people saw it," the other man says cheerily.

"Well, that's very kind of you. I will indeed…be there. At four." I feel like talking *for* this guy. He is driving me crazy. Hand over the controls to me, turtle. Then we'll get some shit done. But then I feel the same sensation I felt in the library, tension and a flush of nervousness. The professor's eyes must be darting around the room because my view is changing as rapidly as TV channels at the mercy of a remote-holding woman.

"OK; see you then!" Ill-Fitting Suit Man chirps as he turns to leave. But he stops when he spots something on the desk. The professor's eyes also go to that spot and I find myself looking at the library book he picked-up earlier. "The Pua Tribe?" Ill-Fitting Suit Man practically yells. "You're reading about the Pua Tribe? What a coincidence, I'm covering that subject next month!" I think for a second that he is going to hug me, or us. He is that excited. I feel the professor's emotions ramping up. More nervousness, anxiety…and maybe something more.

"Oh it's just, it's just…something I picked up…today. At the…the…library. You are, uh, covering it, you say?" he stammers.

"Absolutely. It's a perfect demonstration of cultural appropriation! I didn't know you were interested in anthropology." Ill-Fitting Suit Man raises an eyebrow and steps closer to the desk. My view slides backward as the professor moves his chair back.

"I, why, yes. Yes, I am," the professor manages to say. The tension filling in around me is nearly unbearable. Surely Ill-Fitting Suit Man must notice this, but he seems oblivious. I feel the next emotion now: embarrassment. It is so strong that I want to close my eyes and shut out the feeling.

"Now, don't you go moving in on my job, Alex!" Ill-Fitting Suit Man jokes and heads for the door. The professor struggles to respond but the man is gone by the time he manages to say weakly, "No, no. I…no."

I feel another surge of embarrassment, even stronger than before and want to raise my palms to my cheeks to feel their flush. Nervous waves wash over me uncomfortably. The professor sits still and stares at the spot where Ill-Fitting Suit Man stood. The intense feelings slowly subside, and the tension eases away. What is happening with this guy? Social anxiety disorder? I can feel what he is feeling, but without the benefit of his thoughts to narrate the emotions, it feels disconnected and wrong, somehow. It occurs to me that being able to see his facial expressions would help me decipher what is going on in his head. But that will only happen if he looks in a mirror, just as the little girl almost did.

After sitting through a faculty meeting that bores me even more than the essays, I hitch a ride with the professor to, well, wherever he wants to go. He takes me back to his drab little house, not far from campus. I am not at all surprised that he lives alone. He can barely talk with a librarian, how would a discussion about the Visa bill with a wife go? His home is dull, shabby, and cramped, with teetering stacks of books everywhere. I think of my upscale apartment, trendy furnishings, and expensive art. I would much rather be there, enjoying a glass of wine with a woman, than here in this brown and dying place.

I watch in disgust as he pulls a bottle of cheap vodka off a shelf in the dining room and makes himself a modest drink. I haven't put that brand of vodka in my mouth since high school. I would think a professor would have better taste. He makes a dinner of chicken curry, and for the first time since my ordeal began, I am grateful that I cannot smell.

Throughout the evening, he mumbles to himself, sometimes indistinctly, random and inconsequential vocalizations that do not help me to understand his emotions. At 7:50 p.m. (I know because he looks at the clock on the stove), he sits down at the kitchen table and places the cordless phone in front of him. There is hardly room for it on the table among the piles of books and papers. I wait for him to place a call, but he simply sits and stares out the window at the dimly lit back porch. After a few minutes, the phone rings jarringly in the silence, and if I could have jumped, I would have. The professor reaches for the phone and places it to his ear after pressing a noticeably worn "On" button. What I hear next surprises me. A woman's voice fills my head. It is just as if I am talking on the phone except the voice completely surrounds me. I welcome the break in the professor's bland life and listen raptly.

"Hi, Dad!"

"Hello, Sherry!" the professor's voice fills with joy. I can feel him smile. "I've been...waiting for you to call. Hoped...I hoped you would."

"You know I always call on Tuesdays, Dad!" Her voice is pleasant and light and she sounds happy.

"Indeed. I was thinking about you all day...how did the marathon go?"

"Great! I finished in twenty-seven forty, which is better than last year by three minutes. Good God, it was so hard though. My calf started to cramp near the end, and I wasn't sure I was going to make it," Sherry says.

"I'm so very proud. So proud...of you," he says softly. "You were always so gifted in...athletics."

"Thanks, Dad. How are you doing? What's new at the university?" I listen closely to try to determine if Sherry is good looking or not. So far I am picturing her with brown hair, brown eyes, a thin athletic build, and moderately attractive. This perception is a gift of mine, really. A gift that has been fine-tuned and tested over the years.

"Oh, much the same. There was a...protest outside my building last week. Made a horrible racket they did. Couldn't...couldn't really work," he says.

The conversation between the professor and his daughter drags on for what seems like hours to me. They talk about how to fix her sprinkler system, touch on US politics and round it out with detailed observations on the weather. But I do long for the simple act of conversing with someone. I realize now that we take not only the gift of speech for granted but also the fact that we are noticed by people at all. I am in prison, invisible to anyone who looks through the bars.

After the professor hangs up the phone, he watches TV for a bit. I'm grateful for the distraction. I hope he will flip to Cinemax or something like that so I can at least have some eye candy. But I am stuck with reruns of *Frasier*. Later, as he lies in bed with his eyes open, staring out the window at the tree outside, an intense feeling of loneliness comes over me or more accurately, over the professor. The emotion is unmistakable. I feel as if I want to cry, and when my field of vision blurs with a watery shimmer, I think for a moment that I am crying. But then I realize that of course it's his eyes and his tears. As the tears increasingly blur the scene before us, I feel a pain inside somewhere, almost as if my heart is being pinched. I know he is longing for something, needing something, hoping for something, wanting to fill some hole, but without his mind I have no way of knowing what makes him hurt so much. I remember this feeling. I sometimes felt this way when I found myself with no one beside me in bed at night. I never dwelled on the feeling, but rather pushed it back to a recess of my brain to deal with later. It pissed me off, in fact. But the professor does not push the emotions away. I am forced to sink into them and they feel unending. He doesn't get up and read, or watch TV, or make a midnight snack. He just lies there, staring at the spider web of branches outside the window, and I am forced to feel a loneliness deeper than I ever have before.

Even after his eyes close and I hear the deep breathing that indicates sleep, the feelings of loneliness and sadness persist. Yes, they fade somewhat with his consciousness, but surprisingly, some linger with me as I float in the darkness. How might this shape his dreams I wonder? I also wonder if I will see his dreams. I figure anything is possible at this point. I wait in the silence for an image to appear, whatever he is seeing in REM sleep. But the movie never comes. Either he isn't dreaming yet, or this is something I am unable to see in my...situation. This thought lowers my own mood even more as I wonder about all the nights I will have to spend inside someone else with nothing to see and no sleep to be had. It makes me want to move on to someone else. The professor is boring me already. I tell myself I don't care why he is depressed and lonely. His life doesn't matter to me. But...after experiencing his emotions so intimately today, I can't deny that a part of me feels concern for him.

~

The next morning the professor stands on the bathmat toweling himself off after a particularly uncomfortable shower for me in which I saw more of the guy than I wanted to. He moves to the sink and looks up into the mirror. My mind recoils in shock at the reflection. It should be my own but instead is entirely foreign. His homeliness makes me want to look away in distaste. But, forced to keep staring, I cruelly evaluate every part of him. At his age, he could have been proud of his still-thick hair, but it is cut too short on the sides and left longer on top, almost in a bowl cut. There's no way he can lord it over bald men with that haircut. His face is etched deep with wrinkles, and the bags under his eyes are so puffy that I want to politely, or not so politely, suggest surgery to him. He has the sagging jowls of an older man and a turkey neck. His light blue irises reflect the sadness of many years of disappointment or loneliness. I am glad when he turns away from the mirror.

~

My two car trips with the professor still haven't given me much clue as to what part of the country we are in or which university he works at. He lives very close to the campus and takes a back road to a parking lot for the rear entrance to his building. I am disappointed that I still haven't seen the name of the university. I try to look at people's shirts and sweatshirts as the professor passes them in the hall of his building, but his gaze is habitually glued to the floor.

In his office that morning, he mostly reads the book he had checked out of the library the day before. I try to read along but am so bored by the topic that I sigh internally many times over and instead count the word "and" on each page. At one point he grabs a sticky-note and places it under a sentence on a page. He carefully shuts the book and holds it to his side as he gets up from the desk and ventures down the hall. A slow ride up an ancient elevator takes us to the sixth floor. I expect it to grind to a halt at any moment and trap us, making me double-stuck. I can feel him get nervous, and think maybe he is thinking the same thing about the elevator as it creaks, pops, and makes other unnerving sounds. But the nervous feeling remains even as he lumbers down the hall toward an east-facing window through which sunlight streams like a floodlight. I realize that the professor has been relatively free of emotion this morning. Things have felt fairly neutral. It is only this current increase in emotion that highlights this fact.

He slows down, and his breathing becomes fast and shallow. My first thought is that he is having a heart attack. My second thought is: I'm free! But then his emotions hit me full on. The anxiety and nervousness are potent and quickly build. As he reaches an office door with "Professor Martin, PhD, Cultural Anthropology" written on it, he hesitates and his eyes linger on the lettering longer than necessary to read it.

His soft tap on the door is met by silence, and I feel the professor's anxiety increase. He is almost audibly panting. He knocks again and is answered by a muffled "Come in" from within the office. We open the door to find Ill-Fitting-Suit Man seated at his desk—Professor Martin, I should say. Christ, can't I at least see some new people while we are out? Professor Martin has another bad suit on today and is surrounded by mounds of papers. He smiles at us, crying out, "Alexander! Please come in."

The professor shuffles forward and doesn't say anything. Professor Martin tries harder. "What can I do for you today?" When my professor still fails at speech, Professor Martin's eyes alight on the book I can just barely see being held out in front of me at the bottom edge of my vision.

"Oh, uh, yes," he begins in his usual fashion, which makes me want to roll my eyes. "I, uh, I was reading and came upon, well…I came upon a, a certain premise that I had a…a question about," he finishes, sounding short of breath. Professor Martin's eyes light up.

"Yes! So you've started reading the book! Please sit down, I'd be happy to discuss it with you." He motions to the chair in front of his desk and hastily clears some space on his desk. Although I can't feel it, I am willing to bet that my professor's heart is beating at a frantic pace in his chest. The feelings of anxiety are alarmingly strong. He lowers himself into the chair, opens the book to the page with the sticky-note, and places it in front of Professor Martin with shaky hands.

"I was, uh…curious about the argument that the uh…inhabitants, uh, used objects to supplement their uh…well, their vocabulary."

"Ah, yes!" Professor Martin is nearly orgasmic at the thought of this discussion. But I miss out on the rest of his excited sentences as I focus on where my professor is looking. Instead of looking at the book where Professor Martin is pointing, he is staring unwaveringly at the man's lips. As Professor Martin speaks, I watch uncomfortably as my forced, fixed gaze wanders over his face. The other professor has no idea his face is being mapped, because he is reading from the book. When he glances up to meet our eyes, I feel a jolt of electric nerves. My professor straightens up in his chair and looks down at his hands, which are twisting around each other while resting on the desk.

Professor Martin continues with his monologue, and I begin to wonder if my guy is listening either. With pounding anxiety my gaze again goes up to the man across the desk. He is looking at the book, speaking quickly, and flipping hurriedly through the pages to find another passage to read aloud. We watch the man's eyes, and our gaze keeps returning to the lips that seem to move in slow motion to form each syllable. This incessant staring is making me very uncomfortable, and I would do anything to look away. I wonder if this is just another facet of the professor's social awkwardness. Soon, his gaze drops to the man's neck. The skin there is smooth, much younger than my professor's, and slightly tanned. I remember a woman once telling me that the best way to tell someone's age is by how their neck looks.

Professor Martin looks up at us repeatedly as he speaks, and each time my gaze is dizzily jerked away nervously and down to the book. When I find myself once again watching the other man's lips, I suddenly remember something I read once about body language. When we are attracted to someone, we unconsciously look at their lips because, even if we don't know it yet, we want to kiss them. The realization hits me just as my professor looks at something else on the man: the wedding ring on his left hand. Suddenly the feelings of anxiety and nervousness translate into something entirely different, so foreign to me, in this context. My mind reels as I watch the scene unfold. I hear my professor clear his throat, watch him wipe sweat from his temples, and fidget uncontrollably. I am pulled from my analysis when Professor Martin sits back in his chair and turns toward his computer screen.

"Come look at this, Alexander. I refer to this site often, and it might help explain this concept even better. Come look, sorry, I can't easily turn this monitor," Professor Martin is pulling up a website, and my professor slowly gets up from his chair and makes his way around the desk like an inmate on his way to the gas chamber. Oh boy, I think. My professor stands far back from Professor Martin's chair, taking advantage of his turned back to stare at the back of the man's neck, where the hair is neatly trimmed in a straight line.

"Now look here, see this diagram? See, Alexander, the upward trend in the graph?" Professor Martin turns around and motions my professor in closer, leaning to the side so he can see the screen. I hear my professor's feet shuffle on the plastic floor mat as he moves closer. I start to feel his anxiety seep through. His nervous breathing has to be noticeable, but Professor Martin doesn't say anything. My professor tries to focus on the screen, but his eyes are jumping haphazardly to the man and back. Then it happens. I hear my host inhale through his nose ever so softly, yet drawn out, the way you do when you smell something wonderful cooking. Or the way you do when you smell perfume. My view momentarily turns to black as my professor closes his eyes and enjoys the scent he has inhaled. I want to feel embarrassed, but I only feel his emotions. His anxiety subsides slightly as he relaxes.

But Professor Martin hears the inhalation too, and when he turns his head sharply, he sees that my professor's head is too close to his and inclined toward his neck. I can't smell the cologne. But I know it is there. Professor Martin stops talking midsentence and turns with a questioning look. We straighten up so quickly that I think we might fall over.

"Are you all right, Alexander?" Professor Martin has now lost the childlike excitement in his voice. It is replaced with something I know well: skepticism and disgust. My professor backs away and around the desk so hastily that he bumps into something behind us, and I hear ceramic rattle noisily in the silence. Calm is replaced by anxiety. His constantly darting eyes add to the feeling of chaos. They are like restless insects looking for a place to land.

"What's that? Oh...why, yes...yes, quite. Thank you. Thank you for taking the uh, well, the time to discuss this with me. I really have to, uh...well I really must be going now." I am embarrassed for him as he clumsily heads for the door. And even though I can't see Professor Martin's face, I know he knows. Or at least it is dawning on him. But the part that really bothers me, deep in my invisible core, is that I can feel disgust radiating from Martin and sinking into my professor's back.

He returns to his office, mumbling to himself, not all of it making sense, filled with excruciating shame, regret, and immense sadness. I have never felt sadness of this magnitude before.

~

Later, the professor has a class to teach. He arrives at the midsized classroom fifteen minutes earlier than any student does and uses the time to review his lesson plan. As he stands in silence at the podium and reads his messy handwritten notes, I try not to think about the immense emotional pain he, and I, had been in just hours earlier.

A curious thing happens in those moments before the first group of students arrives. I start to feel sympathy for the professor. I have always been rather disgusted by homosexuality and not at all interested in understanding it. But the pain I feel from the professor doesn't take long for me to decipher it. I know in my core that it's the pain of a broken heart. Having never experienced it before I'm not sure how I know, but it comes through to me none the less. His emotions burn with some of the same feelings I received from Jenny: rejection and loneliness among them. I feel bad for the guy but wonder if my sympathy is due to his emotions taking over me.

As the students come into the room, I immediately recognize how well the professor is liked. Many take the time to smile and say hi to him. Some stop to talk about their experiences or the last topic he has covered. My mood starts to improve a little as I realize I will at least get to check out the hot college girls. Only now I can't be entirely sure whether I am in charge of my mood or if it is the professor who is feeling better because he is distracted by the class. Either way, I sense a lightness in my mood as more and more people fill the room and low murmurs converge into a symphony of talk. With a glance at his watch, the professor signals that it is time to get started by walking to the whiteboard, picking up a marker, and beginning to write. Immediately, the class quietens down behind us, and I realize this must be his routine. When he turns around, I see students opening notebooks, putting away cell phones, and unzipping backpacks. The professor begins to speak, and it takes a moment for me to realize that something quite amazing is happening. He makes it through four or five sentences before it hits me: he is not stuttering or hesitating in any way. His words flow out steadily and with a certain grace. Gone is his usual nervous manner and repetitiveness, replaced by a confident note. He begins to write on the board, while continuing to talk, perfectly complimenting the words he is writing on the board without either one distracting from the other. I can feel his emotions getting more positive with each passing word. As he goes on they approach elation. He is writing feverishly on the board, only pausing to turn around occasionally and make a point, jabbing the air with the marker. The students respond as if held under a spell by his magic wand and put their pens to paper, or hands to keyboards, and faithfully record his words. His words come out effortlessly, without hitch, and I now know that this is not just his comfort zone but his true destiny. I find myself actually listening to his lecture and trying to understand what he is explaining. The way he speaks about it makes you *want* to listen.

By the end of the class, an hour and fifteen minutes later, the professor's mood has markedly improved, and I feel relieved to be free of the emotional prison we have been locked in for most of the day. I wonder if the professor's teaching is enough to get him through heartbreak. Is it enough for him to hide behind?

He packs his books and papers into his briefcase and, as he is heading for the door, pauses to look out a window overlooking the wintery scene outside. Snow has moved in and is swirling just on top of the pavement in a seductive dance with the wind. I sense his shoulders rising up as he breathes a deep sigh before he slowly moves away from the window and plods unsteadily down the hall.

We make our way across campus, and this time the weather prevents students from greeting the professor. Everyone is hunched against the blowing snow. As he walks, his eyes remain downcast as usual, and my desire to see more of my surroundings goes unfulfilled. But as he approaches a long set of concrete steps, he is forced to glance up to judge the ascent. At that moment, he sees Professor Martin descending the steps toward him, on the other side of the handrail. I hear my professor's breath catch in his throat and see him falter and slow down. He looks down immediately. I can almost feel his blood pressure spike. His eyes look anywhere but directly at Professor Martin, who, by the sound of his shoes on the concrete, is coming close. My professor is nearly hyperventilating now, with short intakes of panicked breath. He is moving in slow motion as he climbs the steps. I hear the other footfalls slow down very close to us, and my professor raises his head with what I can only assume is trepidation. Our eyes meet those of Professor Martin's, and in those two seconds, I feel the stab of pain that my professor experiences in reaction to what he sees there. Professor Martin quickly looks away and, without a word, picks up his pace and hurries onward. Like a rope tied to my feet, I can feel my professor pulling me down again into a bottomless pit. Despair washes over me.

My salvation from the pit comes unexpectedly. With a flash of orange light, everything changes. The blinding light fills me until I can no longer see the steps in front of the professor. I know what is happening and am more prepared this time for the pressure upon me and the loud roar of air around me. I try not to fight the pressure pulling me about, but it's hard not to resist. It pulls and pushes me, and the roar reaches a crescendo and then is silenced as quickly as it started.

8 THE GARDEN

An expanse of white spreads out before me, and at
first I think I am stuck in some in-between world. But
then I see, in the corners of my field of vision, curtain
rods with heavy drapes to my left and the top of a
painting on my right. It takes me a minute but I realize
I'm lying down, staring at a ceiling. I hope for a moment
that maybe I'm back in my body again. But my hopes
are quickly dashed when I realize I can't change my field
of vision at will. I hear soft snoring to my left. The
person I am visiting stirs and turns over. I feel like a
ship has just capsized, overwhelmed with dizziness. But
I am greeted with a new sight: a man lying on his back
in bed, bare chested, with messy hair, deeply asleep. I
am, of course, disappointed this view isn't of a woman.
My host is lying on his or her side, watching this man
sleep. I'd assume I am inside a woman, but my last
adventure has taught me that I can't make such
assumptions. The man looks to be in his mid-fifties, and
is probably considered handsome. He inhales and snorts
rather loudly and my host reaches out a hand and
pushes his shoulder gently. The brief glimpse of red

manicured nails and delicate bone structure tells me I am indeed within a woman. The man awakes at this slight disturbance and sleepily opens his eyes and looks at me. I feel an instinct to stop staring into his eyes, but we are so close to him that there is not much choice. My new existence forces me to feel an intimacy with people I have never met. The man has unusually dark eyes of such a deep brown that his pupils nearly blend into his irises, and his eyes seem black. I've never seen such dark eyes before. But when he smiles at my host, the smile reaches into his eyes and lightens them.

"Morning, lovely." His deep voice is scratchy with sleep.

"Good mornin'," I hear my host say. "Sorry I woke you. I tried to push you softly—you were snoring." She has a slight Southern accent, so slight, it's obvious she hasn't been home for a while.

"I never snore," the man says, smiling again and reaching up to rub his eyes and face. He looks at her. "What's on your agenda today?" he asks. The woman sighs and runs her fingers lightly over her face, as if feeling to see if anything has changed overnight.

"Rachel and Carmen are coming over at one to help me plant the flowers by the south wall. And of course I have a thousand errands to run after that," she says, sounding slightly put out.

"Well, don't feel like you have to get them all done today," he says.

"I want to leave tomorrow open for house-hunting," she replies.

"Oh. Of course." His eyes dart to the ceiling and then back to her.

"You forgot," she says, obviously annoyed.

"Just momentarily. But yes, that will be great," he says and smiles warmly at her.

"We have seven houses lined up. We're going to

need most of the day," she says, all business now.

"Seven. Wow. Yes, yes, that's fine," he says. She must have given him a look. "Well, I better be getting into the office." He sits up and stretches on the side of the bed.

"When will you be back?" she asks, sitting up.

"Probably the usual. Five or six. Saturdays are a little bit lighter, you know."

"I know," she replies in a far-off voice. She stares at his bare back as he stretches, her gaze sliding from his neck to his lower spine. She slowly reaches out her hand and nearly touches his back, but he stands up and walks away. She doesn't say anything, just drops her hand to the bed and runs her fingers over the soft sheets. She stares at her fingernails while he speaks to her.

"Where are those houses?" he asks. She pauses before answering and brings her hand up closer to her face to inspect her nails.

"Sea Crest Hills," she mumbles.

"Sea Crest Hills?" the man repeats with a note of disbelief. The one I reserve for when a woman says something that I find preposterous.

"Yes. They are truly divine homes. You'll see. Wait until you see the yards. They're not suburban yards. They're hilly and natural." She finally looks up at him, but only out of the corner of her eye.

"We can't afford Sea Crest Hills. I've told you that," he says. Now he sounds exasperated. She moves to the edge of the bed and reaches for what looks like a vat of lotion on the bedside table. The way she slowly unscrews the lid, sets it down on the bed, and applies the shiny lotion to the backs of her hands in even strokes reminds me of a robot, programmed for a precision task.

"There are a couple of homes that are just a tad over our budget," she says, "But, when you get your promotion it won't be an issue."

"I don't have it *yet*," he sighs. "We can go look at a few in Sea Crest, but don't get your hopes up."

"Seven," she says again, emphasizing the word, while still rubbing the lotion into her hands and wrists. My keen and judgmental eye notices her wrinkles. There goes my hope that he is with a young, hot woman that I get to see in a mirror. He doesn't answer and finally she looks up at him. He's glaring at her but looks like he can be persuaded. I am right.

"Fine. Seven," he says and throws up his hands. She sits all the way up in bed and more vertigo hits me. But I see more of the room now. It's a large master bedroom with plain white walls full of artwork and furnished in a style I call "stuffy chic." Leopard prints and black velvet abound, the bed is a four-poster mahogany king, there are matching dressers, satin covered chairs, heavy curtains, expensive looking art— the works. I don't hate it, but it is a little much. The man heads for the bathroom and half turns around as he walks.

"That promotion *is* getting close," he says, grinning at her, before closing the bathroom door. She lies back down in bed for a while, staring at nothing, and driving me crazy. She seems to be waiting for him to finish getting ready. I try to get a read on her emotions. I focus on what I'm feeling, what mood I'm in, because of her. I'm not getting much of anything. I feel a faint sense of anxiousness, but it's barely there, and I'm not quite sure that's what it is. Also a feeling of calm. The emotions contradict each other and confuse me. I wait impatiently for other clues.

When he returns he is fully dressed in a suit and tie: Armani. I approve.

"Have a great day. I'll see you tonight," he says as he fastens his watch. A Rolex. Ah, I miss mine. I think he is coming toward her for a kiss, but he grabs his cell phone off the bedside table instead.

"You too," she replies lazily as she stretches across the bed and watches him. I have the notion that she is waiting for him to leave in order for something to happen. She seems to be lingering in the bed, yet coiled tight, ready to spring up. My first thought is an affair. She is behaving like a woman who is having an affair, waiting for her husband to leave the house for the day so that her lover can come ravage her. Her casualness seems almost forced. This could be an interesting day.

"I love you," her husband says as he walks out the door, throwing a quick smile her way.

"I love you too," she says. Perhaps it is my love of all things dirty and sinful, but I would have sworn it was the most loaded "I love you" I have ever heard. I sit back, metaphorically, to enjoy the show.

She springs from the bed the moment he leaves, and for once I get a good look at my host soon after joining her. She strides purposely to the bathroom and leans in over the counter to look closely at her face in the mirror, staring at herself for so long that I begin to get uncomfortable. Next, she pulls out an accordion mirror mounted on the wall and brings a magnifying mirror to her face. I am terrified and fascinated. She and I inspect every inch of her face for much longer than I believe is necessary. I never knew there was so much to worry about on a face. She runs her fingertips lightly over her wrinkles and mutters to herself about her blemishes. She pulls her skin taut to mimic what it must have looked like when she was younger and without wrinkles. I am suddenly very glad I was born male and never worry about those things.

I estimate her age at about forty-five, but she could be fooling me, because I glimpsed the cosmetic product lineup on the bathroom counter, and I am guessing they are not from Walmart. She has a regal face and is quite beautiful. Her cheekbones are high, her nose straight, and her lips are full but not too full. She has the usual crow's feet and forehead wrinkles, but otherwise she seems to be aging gracefully. She doesn't have visible laugh lines though, and her eyes are tired and old. She is wearing cotton pajamas in leopard print and reaches up and starts unbuttoning the top while still watching herself in the mirror. But she soon turns around and heads for the diagonal shower stall in the corner of the bathroom. She undresses by the shower and carefully hangs her pajamas on a hook next to the shower door. I get the feeling everything she does is part of a careful routine. I feel I am invading her privacy, and it makes me uncomfortable. I want to be excited that I am going to shower with a woman; I can't deny who I am at my core. But somehow my instincts are tempered by the knowledge that she has not given me permission to be here.

She takes a long shower, applying more products than I have ever seen anyone use. I catch glimpses of her body as she goes about her routine, because I have no choice. She seems to be in good shape and obviously takes care of herself. But I feel creepy and cannot understand the purpose of my being here and witnessing this. When she is done, she dries off and puts a robe on without ever glancing over toward the large mirrors that surround the long counter and sinks. That surprises me. I had expected her to spend as long gazing at her body as she had at her face. I feel strangely conflicted about missing the opportunity to stare, yet not feeling right about it either.

While she is applying her makeup, a phone in the bedroom rings, and she stops to answer it. "Hi, Gwen," the caller, a woman with a high-pitched and hyper voice, says before prattling on about her day. I am disappointed to realize that it's her friends who are coming over—no steamy affair after all. Phone call over, Gwen hurries through the rest of her makeup and dresses quickly. Her friend had said she would be there in half an hour.

The bedroom leads onto a second floor landing with a balcony that looks out over a giant living room below. Two sets of stairs curve down in an arc from either side of the balcony. I like the opulence already. An enormous stone fireplace rising from the floor to the ceiling dominates the living room. Tall windows on the adjacent wall let in plenty of light. As she descends the stairs to the left, the room gradually comes into view. The décor here reflects a more masculine taste, and I like it better than the bedroom. Some decent art hangs on the wall, several sculptures are scattered around, and a small bar is setup in the corner of the living room with a martini shaker glinting in the sun. It is much more to my taste than the professor's drab house. For a moment, Gwen pauses on the stairs, and looks out over the living room. Everything seems quiet and in its place. The uneven movement down the curved stairs makes me feel sick, and I realize I now have to get used to another person's walk.

I have plenty to look at as Gwen moves into the kitchen, her eyes darting everywhere. She's very different from the professor who always looked down at the ground. Gwen's eyes fall on cherry cabinets, granite countertops, and beautiful glass dishware displayed on shelves and counters. Beyond the kitchen, through the window, I see the generic manufactured landscaping of a suburban lawn. Everything in the kitchen is in its place. Everything is spotless. I watch with interest as Gwen retrieves the fixings for bloody marys, methodically chopping the celery into perfect leaf-topped stalks. She glances at the clock. It's 9:55 a.m. I like the way these people live.

~

Rachel and Carmen arrive at ten o'clock sharp, announcing themselves with a ring of the doorbell. They look like they belong behind the makeup counter at Bloomingdales. They are so perfectly done up, with clothes so achingly fashionable, that I wonder if this can really be how they always dress to visit a friend at ten on a Saturday morning. There is much kissing of cheeks and hugs that barely touch as the women greet each other. They waste little time making the bloody marys and move to the deck to sit under the umbrella. Once settled they launch into conversation, as old friends do. They are comfortable and relaxed with each other, jumping from topic to topic so quickly my mind reels: Rachel's daughter's dance class; Gwen's house-hunting plans; Carmen's post-surgery infection. I gather it was breast implants not only by the look of them but by the motions she makes toward the underside of her right breast. I shudder when she mentions a tube. I watch their perfectly colored lips as they speak and their hand gestures, which seem somehow clichéd. After what seems like hours, and another round of drinks, they finally ask Gwen where the flowers and gardening tools are. I had forgotten that was the point of the gathering. I'm surprised they would give up drinking for gardening. But it doesn't last long. They perch primly on little foam knee pads and plant four small flowers in a bed, then stand up and grab their drinks and talk some more. When the talking slows, Gwen goes inside to make more drinks. They plant a few more flowers and then talk again.

"So, Rick has this fantasy for us to have sex at someone else's house during a cocktail party," Carmen says while stirring her drink with her celery and rolling her eyes. *Now* I'm listening—and taking the opportunity to check out her body as Gwen stares at her. The implants accentuate Carmen's tiny waistline, adding to the hourglass effect. Her body looks young in clothes, but her face betrays her. Her too-tanned skin only highlights her wrinkles. I try to decide if I would sleep with her if given the chance.

"Oh my God—why?" Rachel asks, laughing.

"He says it would really turn him on." Carmen shrugs.

"Well, you are *not* doing it at my house on the twenty-ninth! I could never look at my bathrooms the same, wondering which one you were in." Rachel screeches with laughter.

"Ick." Carmen scrunches her face in disgust. "Why would it be in a bathroom? I was thinking a guest bedroom or something."

"I don't know," Rachel says. "I just assume that's where you would have sex in someone else's house, for some reason. Maybe because you know that no one will walk in."

"Well, I think that's part of what he likes about it! That someone could walk in!" Carmen looks mischievous. "Gwen—what do you think? Should I do it?"

Gwen looks away and plants another flower halfheartedly. There is a pause as she pulls off her gardening gloves and looks up at them.

"At Rachel's house? Absolutely."

Rachel shrieks and pretends she is going to throw her celery at Gwen. They all dissolve into laughter. But I don't feel from Gwen any of the emotions that usually come with laughter. I concentrate and try to be fully aware. But there is no joy, no happiness, nothing that matches her outward mood. Now her laughter sounds fake and hollow to me.

By now they have decided they have had enough gardening for the day. Carmen and Rachel turn and go back up on the deck, laughing and swaying in their Christian Louboutins. Finally I am hit by a strong emotion from Gwen. She stops and stands stiffly, staring at a new flower, just planted. I can't be sure about what I'm feeling, at first she seems sad, but as her gaze follows her friends, it becomes recognizable: jealousy. At first I think she might be envious of their footwear, since her gaze has just been on their expensive shoes. But the last topic of conversation had triggered the emotion.

The bloody mary ladies stay a little while longer, and the talk is never dull. I feel like I have been given a back-stage pass to Estrogenville, where there is a three-drink minimum. I learn many things I have always wanted to know about women and a few things I never wanted to know. I also learn some things about these women: they do not work outside the home, they prefer it that way, and they like to brag about their opulent lives.

When Carmen and Rachel leave, Gwen wanders around the house with all the enthusiasm of a death-row inmate in her cell. She drags herself from room to room, slowly running her hands over the furniture, taking in all the art and furniture, but I can tell by her slow walk and the way her gaze lingers on certain things that she isn't really seeing anything. There is nothing for her to do, nothing for her to straighten up or organize. Throughout the house, everything is in its place, as if it were a show home just waiting for prospective buyers. I feel uncomfortable as she moves silently from room to room, on autopilot. Her mind feels blank to me. I feel nothing. No emotions. She ends up in the master bathroom and opens up a silk box on the counter and retrieves a prescription pill bottle. The label is turned around in her hand, and I can't see what the medication is. She slowly and methodically takes one pill with water, replaces the bottle precisely where it had been inside the fancy box, and closes the box with a soft click. That one pill came with more foreboding than if she had taken the whole bottle. I know there is more to Gwen than meets the eye.

~

The afternoon is filled with errands. The changing scenery and interaction with other people proves incredibly entertaining for me. Gwen is the epitome of kindness and social grace in public. Everyone she meets is greeted as an old friend, and perhaps they all are. But once back in her Mercedes GL550, she lapses into silence. I will admit that I talk to myself when alone. Just mutterings about what I am doing at the moment or exclamations of joy or incredulity while watching the daily stock-market report. But Gwen doesn't talk to herself at all. Perhaps she is normal, and I am the odd one. I don't know. Occasionally, at stoplights, she looks at her reflection in the rearview mirror or even pulls down the visor for a better look. But she doesn't do any of the usual things that I have seen women do in cars. No lipstick is applied; her lips are already perfect. No powder; she has no unsightly shine. She just turns her head slightly from side to side and studies herself. Her expression is always blank; her emotional plane muted.

I have been waiting all day for a clue as to what city we are in and I am rewarded when the Space Needle comes in to view. Seattle is as beautiful as I remember. Memories come flooding back to me of a weekend I spent here a few years back. I had met Shannon online and engaged in enthusiastic flirting, cybersex, and phone sex for two months before she suggested we meet in person and see if we had relationship potential. I knew we didn't. She was just a nice distraction after work as I sat on my balcony with a scotch, the laptop on a table in front of me. She seemed ditzy, and her little girly voice did nothing for me, so I often told her it was much sexier to be quiet when we used the webcam. I didn't even feel guilty that I was also dating a woman in my own city at the time. Online dating was different. It was surreal. It was fantasy land. That was my reasoning, and it worked well for me. When Shannon wanted to meet, I tried at first to come up with excuses. But she was persistent, and I had to admit that I was curious about what she was like in the flesh. So I left fantasy land and flew out for the weekend to reality in Seattle. After a few hours in her bed in her cramped downtown studio apartment, I insisted we go to the Four Seasons. She thought I was being romantic. But I just couldn't stand her limp, pilled sheets and plastic dishware. We spent time walking around Seattle, me treating her to expensive drinks and dinners, clothes, and even a delicate vase she had gushed about in an antique store. The sex was great. She thought it was love. She left me at the airport with glistening eyes and a wide grin. I grinned back and waved as I thought about where to eat that night. I got on the plane and called my other girl, Mandy, to tell her how my business trip went. Once home I deleted my online profile from the dating site; blocked Shannon's e-mails, IMs, Skype, and phone number; and never spoke to her again. It was neat, clean, and extremely bastardly. I don't know why I did those things. For me to point to my father is much too easy. Although he is always in the front of mind when I examine my destructive behaviors, which isn't often, I must admit. When Mandy found out about not Shannon but another woman later, instead of cutting me loose, she begged for me to get counseling so we could get through my problem together. I promptly dumped her. To me it was simple: women needed to fit into my life and realize exactly how it worked for me. If it got complicated, I moved on.

I am brought back to Gwen when she starts speaking. She is talking into the phone via the Bluetooth in her car.

"Darling, I'll be driving by the dry cleaners in about five, are your shirts ready?" she asks without so much as a hello. Her husband's voice comes through the microphone above us.

"Uh, well, no," he answers. Gwen pauses, manicured nails tapping on the shellacked wood steering wheel.

"But you dropped them off days ago!" she cries, annoyed.

"Well what I meant was, they aren't ready at *that* dry cleaners." Once again Gwen pauses for a moment after his response.

"Then at which dry cleaners might they be, Robert?" Her voice has a sharp edge to it now.

"The one on Union Street," he answers quietly. This time there is no pause before Gwen speaks.

"I see. Then I trust you will pick them up on your way back from seeing your whore. See you for dinner." She punches the button on the steering wheel and cuts the connection. *Now* Gwen is speaking my language! I knew someone was having an affair. Seems to me that every marriage has at least one, whether both parties know about it or not. I smile to my cynical self. Of course, I also know that Gwen could be acting irrationally and accusing her husband of something that is untrue. She did cut him off before he had time to respond. I watch as Gwen continues to drive in silence. Nothing suggests a bad mood or even the sharp words of a moment before. No heavy foot on the gas pedal, no reckless turns, no swearing or calling a best friend to vent, and, most notably, no emotions pumping through her brain to me. Nothing. I wait for an outburst of an emotion from her that never comes.

~

Back at her home, which is just as impressive to see from the driveway as from inside, Gwen begins cooking dinner the minute she walks in the door. She is moving so quickly around the kitchen I get slightly dizzy. She switches on the small flat screen TV in the corner of the cabinet and turns it to a cooking show. I watch as she prepares an Italian dish with risotto and realize that I truly miss eating. I wish I could smell the simmering sauce that she is stirring. As she is setting the table, Robert comes home and I hear him go straight upstairs. A plastic crinkling noise follows him that sounds distinctly like packaged shirts from the dry cleaner. The one on Union Street, of course.

Gwen fills the plates and waits in the kitchen, leaning back against a counter top and drinking a glass of red wine, still watching the cooking show. But I'm not sure she's actually watching it. Her stare is unblinking and the TV screen goes out of focus. I still have no read on her emotions. Robert comes into the room, his hair damp from a shower. Gwen glances at him out of the corner of her eye.

"Perfect timing. Everything is on the table," she says, without warmth. She takes her glass to her spot at the table, facing the living room. Robert's place is set at the head of the table.

"This looks delicious," Robert says. The compliment sounds genuine, but his voice is flat.

"Thank you. It's one of Carmen's recipes."

"Carmen doesn't cook." A slight smile turns up the

corner of his mouth.

"Well then, it's her chef's recipe. I don't know, Robert," Gwen says with a sigh.

"Gwen…" He stops and looks at her.

"Not now, Robert."

"Yes now, Gwen," he says firmly, as if to a child. "Why did you say what you said on the phone earlier? I thought we were past that."

I mentally sit back, grab some popcorn, and get ready to watch entertaining dinner theater.

"Some days, Robert…it just bubbles up," Gwen says, staring at her risotto.

Robert is quiet for a moment and seems to think about that. "I understand. I know it's hard. Do you want me to stop seeing her?" When she finally looks up at him, I see genuine concern in his eyes.

"No, no, I…I don't want that. We have an agreement, and this is what we do. I just let my emotions get the best of me today. I'll be OK," she says with determination. I am thoroughly confused.

"Are you absolutely sure, Gwen? Yes, we have an agreement, but it's not set in stone. Things can always change."

"Except that they can't, Robert. They don't change, and they won't. I'm still the same. And this is what works. Please, let's drop it now, and enjoy our dinner." She continues to eat and must have smiled at him because he hesitantly smiles back and then takes a long swallow of wine.

"OK," he says quietly and sets his glass down with a clink.

The dinner theater isn't nearly as much fun as I had hoped it would be. Instead, I am left with an empty Gwen, devoid of feeling. I have a better idea now about what is going on but still don't know the cause. Obviously, Robert has a mistress, and Gwen not only allows it but seems to encourage it, at least sometimes. I wonder why. If she is jealous of the affair, why would she insist that he keep carrying it on?

~

Robert goes to bed around eleven-thirty, saying goodnight to Gwen before he leaves the living room. She stays up to watch *Discovery Health* until nearly two in the morning. This happens night after night. Robert goes to bed first; Gwen never goes with him. They say good night pleasantly enough but never hug, kiss, or so much as touch each other. Smiles are exchanged, but there is only emptiness and sterility behind them. They never make love, never even come together in the middle of the king-sized bed.

~

I have spent much more time with Gwen than with the other two. By my calculation it has now been roughly two months. I see the date when she opens the calendar on her phone and often watch her write the date on checks. I get to know Gwen, even to like her, and, playing against type, feel sorry for her. Nothing has changed. She and Robert's marriage remains the same tired charade. Robert did not get his big promotion after all and the house hunting came to an abrupt halt. Gwen had behaved like a spoiled child; whining about Sea Crest Hills any chance she got. I could tell it only pushed Robert further away.

No one else seems to know about their agreement. Gwen talks about sex with the bloody mary ladies when they get together every week, seeming to relate experiences she'd had just the evening before with Robert. But I know the truth. There's no hiding from me. At cocktail parties she and Robert make a lovely couple for the outside observer. And I can tell that they are well liked in their circle of friends and among Robert's colleagues. They haven't talked about Robert's extramarital activities since that night at dinner. But I can always tell, as I'm sure Gwen can, when he is going to see his mistress. It is usually on a Saturday and Robert's plans for the day are vague. He also always takes a shower as soon as he comes home.

Gwen quietly lives her life on an island to which she seems to have sailed herself. Most evenings end on the couch watching *Discovery Health*. She has me hooked on it now, too. Not that I have a choice. Although, it wouldn't kill her to switch over to HBO once in a while. Night after night we watch ridiculous but riveting stories of obesity, pregnancy abnormalities, rare tumors, nocturnal binging, or brain trauma. Gwen makes herself a cocktail, and she and I have our Discovery date. I join in her loneliness. When she exclaims aloud about something on the screen, she sometimes turns her head to look around the room, as if to see if anyone else has seen it, only to remember that no one else is there. I can tell she wants someone to talk to while she watches TV. I grow so lonely that I wish she and I could communicate. *"Yes! Yes."* I would say to her emphatically. *"That is some fucked up shit. Nine hundred pounds. Fuck. He's not even trying to lose weight. Look at what he's eating—grilled cheese. And why do you think this doctor is the only one that will perform the surgery? He just wants to be on TV. The other ones know he will just go back to his same disgusting-ass habits afterward."* We could talk about how messed up these people's lives are and feel better about ours. But I also long for real conversation and to make Gwen laugh. She doesn't laugh often, and her lack of emotions seem to be taking a toll on me. I crave not only conversation but to *feel* something.

When she goes to bed, she quietly eases onto the mattress, careful not to disturb Robert. But if she does occasionally, I notice he turns over and seems to reach for her in his half sleep. She will stop and stare at his outstretched hand but lie down just out of reach. When she sleeps, I can feel some emotions that are probably linked to her dreams. She occasionally cries out "No," and sometimes is fearful—perhaps running from an unknown pursuer. But sometimes she seems to have erotic dreams, and this puzzles me more than anything else. I recognize them by what I can read from her inner being. Her usual melancholy melts away and is replaced by a warm, embracing, and pleasurable feeling. Her breathing becomes shallow, and she moans. I feel her becoming more satisfied as if she is giving herself over to a primal feeling inside. Oh, how I want to be able to see what she is seeing. I welcome her occasional departures into the sexual dream realm as vacations from her usual depression. But I also wonder why she is erotic in her dreams but not in her waking life when a man is lying two feet away from her. A man who, I have to now admit, is a good man. A better man than I am. He is good and kind to Gwen. It sounds a little ridiculous, considering he is having an affair, but I have seen enough to know that he truly loves Gwen and that there is more going on than I know.

I wonder just how long I will stay with Gwen and what determines the length of time I spend with these people. I keep waiting for that feeling of being yanked away. But of course, that happens when I least expect it. I don't mind being with Gwen. She lives in a nice, comfortable place, but I worry that she will suck me down into her emotional pit and that if I stay with her much longer I will never get out. But fear of the unknown also unnerves me. I don't know who I will join next. I will have to get used to another life, a new walk, and new emotions.

~

This evening, as Gwen and I sit on the couch, cocktail in hand, we stay up even later than usual watching episode after episode of *Discovery Health* that she had recorded earlier in the week, missed because of a charity banquet and a dinner party with Robert. As she comes to the last recorded episode she clicks to view the episode overview. I read the description along with her. "Altering Sexual Response. Sarah is treated for excessive sex drive. Linda is treated for lack of sexual desire." Gwen stares at the screen longer than is necessary to read the words. She is still for a few seconds, then clicks "Watch Now." At that precise moment, I think I feel a twinge of emotion from her. It is brief, but I think it might be nervousness.

The episode starts out with Sarah, and let me tell you, it is goddamned fascinating. But it makes me miss sex like crazy. Sarah is hooked up to computers that scan her brain waves, neurological responses, body temperature, and God knows what else. They determine that something in her brain has triggered her overactive sexual responses. I am not really listening, I am just watching Sarah as the doctors have her view sexy images on a screen. The woman looks like she is in heat and will start scratching the walls any second. Gwen watches in silence, sitting completely still on the couch. Her neglected Manhattan sits on the coffee table. She fast-forwards through the commercials. Sarah is on a clinical trial for a new drug that will even out her sexual response. Just as the thought crosses my mind that this woman is crazy for wanting to dampen something as carnal as this, they show Sarah inconspicuously rubbing up against a metal pole in line at the airport, and it is rather disturbing. OK, maybe she does need some help.

In the second half of the show, we meet Linda, and Gwen seems to find this even more interesting, although I don't. Gwen's emotions push through her prescription-induced mental fog, and I feel the nervousness again and maybe even anxiety. Linda is fifty-two years old and had a hysterectomy two years ago. She has been left with absolutely no sexual desire, and since this is common after a surgery such as this, she takes hormones to mitigate the effect. But they do nothing for her, and she has been left frustrated for years as her relationship with her husband has degraded. The camera zooms in as tears roll down her face, and she describes how awkward things have become between her and her husband. Gwen leans forward and pulls a nearby throw pillow into her lap, wrapping her arms around it. Emotions surge through her like tidal waves. And suddenly, belatedly—like the man I am—I understand. Gwen starts to cry. Her vision blurs as her eyes fill with tears and then momentarily clears as they fall away, only to blur again with the next round. She delicately swipes at her eyes with manicured fingers but still doesn't move from the couch. The show goes into more detail about what Linda has tried. To my surprise the doctors give Linda the same drug they tried with Sarah. This drug can even out and balance the sex drive and response, increasing low desire, dampening down high. Gwen is riveted to the screen; her tears are drying up. Linda is shown coming in for another appointment with the doctor and sharing the good news that the medicine is making a difference for her. She smiles and laughs as she recounts her experience with happy disbelief. She says her life is changed.

Gwen dissolves into a sobbing mess. I have never felt her like this before. She sobs herself into hiccups, and her hands shake. I feel emotional pain coming through her, the kind that comes from a deep release after holding something back for a long time. The show ends with upbeat music, signaling a problem solved, and then there is abrupt silence in the room as the recorder returns to the main screen. Gwen's sobs abate, and she wipes again at her eyes and face, sniffling and taking deep breaths. She sighs when she sees the smeared makeup on her hands. True to form, she heads directly for the half bath to straighten up her face. Returning to the couch, she takes a big drink of her Manhattan, then replays the episode and fast-forwards until she finds the part where the narrator names the experimental drug. She writes it down, turns off the TV, and stands for a long time staring out the living room windows at the small waterfall in the backyard, lit up by strategically placed spotlights. I am confused when I feel a new emotion slam into me. I don't recognize it at first and have to concentrate to identify it. As she turns from the window and begins turning off lights to go to bed, I know what it is: hope.

~

Gwen still feels hopeful the following morning. This is the best I've felt with her. Robert is gone when she awakes, so I don't know if she would have told him about her plan had he been there. Gwen calls her gynecologist as soon as the clock says 9:00 a.m. After politely asking, and then demanding, that she speak to Dr. Freeman, she is told by a now pissed-off receptionist that the doctor will call her back in between his next appointments. Gwen doesn't hang up before letting the woman know that she and Robert donate substantial amounts of money to the hospital every year.

For the next hour, Gwen paces the house so much that I am as dizzy as when I'd first met her. She picks uncharacteristically at the polish on her thumbnail, leaving it in shreds and apparently not caring. A bloody mary takes the edge off, and she sits down for a bit. I can feel the anticipation pumping through her and am surprised at myself when I realize that every part of me, or what is left of me, is rooting for her. I become just as anxious as she. Or is it that *I am* as anxious as she? It is hard to tell any more.

The phone rings at 10:05 a.m. and Gwen nearly knocks her glass over when she jumps up from the table.

"Hello?" She holds the phone with both hands. I can see both her bent elbows when she glances down at the floor and listens.

"Gwen. It's Dr. Freeman," a man with a gentle voice says in her ear and my head.

"Thank you for returning my call, Doctor. I really do appreciate it."

"Pam said you sounded rather upset, Gwen. Is everything all right?"

"Have you heard of Phonaphal?" she asks, getting right to the point. There is a pause. Gwen lowers one hand to lay it flat on the granite countertop. I try to imagine its cool touch.

"Well. Yes, I have. I see now why you are calling."

"Well, honestly, you should have been the one calling me as soon as you learned of this new drug. This could be the answer for me, Doctor," Gwen tries to sound miffed, but the tremor in her voice gives her away. The doctor must pick up on it as well, as he softens his tone.

"Phonaphal is still pending FDA approval, Gwen."

"I figured that, but…" Gwen interrupts.

"The full reports are not even available on it yet."

"I understand, Doctor. But I have tried the hormones. I have tried the creams. You have given me everything you can think of, and yet there's no difference. You're one of the most renowned doctors in Washington; you've been written up in medical journals. I know you can get this drug. And I…I have money. Surely that gets us somewhere." Gwen's voice is steady now. The doctor pauses. She is patient.

"I'll make some calls, Gwen. I might be able to get you in under a clinical trial. That's all I can do at this point."

"Oh, thank you, Doctor. Thank you. It's just that I saw it on *Discovery Health* and it really worked for that woman and I just knew that you would have heard about it." Her words come out quickly, with desperation and relief.

"Yes. The Discovery Channel is responsible for a lot of my office visits," Dr. Freeman says with a sigh. "Listen, Gwen, let me see what I can find out. And when I have news, I want to see you so we can catch up and find out where you are at this point. I haven't seen you in a while." His voice is full of concern now. Gwen breathes out heavily and I can feel her relief.

"Thank you, Dr. Freeman. I just want so much for this to be the answer," she says softly.

"I know, Gwen. You have been through a lot. I truly hope we can help you to feel better."

After Gwen hangs up she walks slowly to the master bathroom and stops in front of the full-length mirror. She stands so long staring into her own eyes that I have the unnerving feeling that she is looking directly at me and knows I'm here. Then, for the first time since I joined her, she allows her eyes to stray past her face. She looks down at her body letting her gaze trail slowly down her frame. Turning slightly, she looks at her back and behind. She gently runs her hands over her collarbone, breasts, ribs, stomach, and thighs. A feeling of hope surges up in her, and I want her to smile, but she still does not. I can guess that she is guarding her hope, holding it to her until she knows it is really OK to let it fly free. Her trance is broken by the ringing of the phone. It's one of the bloody mary ladies. It's time to plant some more flowers in Gwen's garden.

~

Gwen's newfound hope is almost tangible. I can feel it pulsing through her, driving her forward. New emotions spin off from it. Elation. Giddiness. Inspiration. Her body language even seems to change, at least from my perspective. She moves around a little more quickly and with more purpose, as if she has more energy all of a sudden. She hums as she makes the drinks in the kitchen and takes extra time arranging the fresh flowers on the outdoor table. The bloody mary ladies even notice that something is different, but Gwen doesn't give any clues as to why or what she is thinking. I know with certainty that she has never told them about her problems. When Rachel asks if something is on Gwen's mind, Gwen replies that she is excited about the prospect of moving to a new neighborhood.

I am surprised at how this hope has elevated her to a new emotional level. It seems to have opened a door in her mind that had been locked by depression and prescription drugs. I wonder if it is like this for everyone. Could hope really be this strong? I have never been religious and am not one to hope for much. In fact, I think all I ever hoped for was a woman to decide to come home with me and then leave quickly and quietly in the morning. But hope is changing Gwen, even though nothing has happened yet. Just the mere idea, the feeling deep within her, is enough to alter her day-to-day state of being.

That evening Gwen spends extra time making an

elaborate dinner. As she works on each dish it occurs to me that her culinary choices are focused on keeping the diner at the table for as long as possible. Steamed artichokes for appetizers are sure to take a while. The Cornish hens would be a hands-on affair as well. She takes new, white tapered candles from a drawer and places them in elaborate crystal holders on the table. I can feel her hope still buzzing inside her, along with anxiousness and excitement. It's so good to finally be feeling something. It connects me to her in a more tangible way. I realize that I now have hope too. I hope Robert will come home when he says he will and won't call at the last minute to say he is tied up. "Tied up to a bed" is what I always imagine when he uses that phrase. I want this for Gwen. She needs it. I like the new, hopeful Gwen. And, more intimately, I have hope for myself. This could all end well for me. I now have hope that it will.

Robert comes home on time. He expresses surprise at the meal now in its final stages in the kitchen. Gwen asks him to open a bottle of Malbec and then seats herself at the table in front of a plump artichoke and a small crystal dish of garlic butter. I know her heart must be beating wildly even though I can't feel that part of her. She looks down at her diamond ring and twists it around and around her finger. Halfway through the artichokes, which I long to taste, partway through the first glass of Malbec, which I long to smell, at the beginning of polite conversation, Gwen wipes her hands and sits back.

"Robert?"

"Mm?" He is savoring an artichoke leaf with his eyes closed.

"I was wondering if you would stop seeing her," Gwen says. The way she says it, it's not a question but a statement. I wish all women were this direct. Robert's eyes snap open, and his hand freezes, leaf in midair.

"Where is this coming from, Gwen?" Robert's voice is soft. He dabs at his mouth with his napkin. Gwen sits forward in her seat, and I hear her take a deep breath.

"There's a new prescription medication, Robert. One designed just for...women like me."

I feel like she is smiling a little. Robert raises his eyebrows.

"It seems like we've been told that before, and they have not been helpful," Robert says delicately.

"I know. But those were hormones. This is a new medication, and it was featured on *Discovery Health* and..." Gwen is talking fast but pauses as Robert's shoulders slump slightly at the mention of the TV show.

"Gwen," Robert's voice is gentle.

"And it really works, Robert," she continues. "I called Dr. Freeman today, and he said it's still undergoing the final testing and approval, but it could be an option for me."

"You...already called him?" Robert asks, leaning forward. "And...*Discovery Health*...Gwen." He sounds skeptical.

"Yes, it was featured on *Discovery Health*. It's a perfectly reputable source, Robert. Dr. Freeman knew what the drug was right away." Her voice is a little haughty. She stares him directly in the eye. Yet I can picture the desperation that must show on her face as well. Robert's face softens.

"Well, the testing and approval part is a little scary, but I guess every drug has to go through that. Dr. Freeman really thinks it might be right for you?"

"Yes. It's completely new, and on the show they explained that they had isolated the hormone that affects...well, you know...and have learned what the right combination is so it will be effective. You should have seen this woman, Robert; it changed her life,"

Gwen trails off and speaks the last part softly.

"As long as it's safe and the side effects aren't too bad, then by all means let's move forward with Dr. Freeman," Robert smiles warmly at her. I can feel Gwen's relief wash over her and bring her peace. And I feel what I know to be happiness come over her. It has been so long since I have felt it that it takes me a moment to identify it. It is like she is being opened up and given light. It is a pretty amazing feeling actually.

"And Gwen?" Robert says as he leans forward further and takes her hand on top of the table. I feel a jolt of emotion go through Gwen at this small but significant contact. "I will most certainly stop seeing her."

Now, you can't bullshit a bullshitter, and I am definitely a bullshitter. I watch for the signs in Robert's eyes, mouth, and body language. I am extremely relieved for Gwen when I determine that he is telling the truth.

They hold hands for a while longer as Gwen talks more about the show and how she'd like him to watch it with her. They talk more during that dinner than they have done in the whole time I've been there. They talk like they are on vacation. It is the kind of relaxed discussion that flows anywhere easily and serves to reconnect people. I can plainly see that while Gwen and Robert have essentially been living separate emotional lives, they remain connected by what is vital: love. They do love and genuinely respect each other. In Robert's eyes and Gwen's tone of voice I can see and hear their shared past.

~

After dinner they go straight to the TV to watch the episode together. They sit on the same couch but still with their usual buffer of distance. The wall will fall but is only just now crumbling. Gwen fast-forwards to the second part of the episode and holds her wine glass tightly in front of her. As Linda explains her struggle and her husband looks on with concern and love, Gwen starts to cry. Quietly at first and without wiping away her tears, perhaps so that Robert won't notice. But soon she leans forward and puts her head in her hands and begins to sob. My view is cut to black as she closes her eyes, and I can only hear and feel her pain. I will never know just how long Gwen has struggled or how long their marriage has been strained. I will never know the depth of her inner shame and depression. She, and her medications, have hidden them well. I'm sure even her closest friends have never known. She has suffered in silence. And today I can feel an enormous amount of pent-up energy being let loose. It is overwhelming. It is so much more than has ever come from her, and really so much more than I have ever felt myself in my life. I didn't know you could *feel* this much all at once. It crosses my mind that maybe this is how all women are, and I'm just now getting to understand it. It would explain a lot…and makes me really glad to be a man.

I am not aware that Robert has come to sit right next to her until she removes her hands from her eyes and I see his leg pressed against the side of hers. She leans into him, and I think that his right arm is probably around her shoulders. Her face is pressed against his collarbone, and Robert gently touches her cheek with his left hand. It is so tender a moment that I once again feel like I am intruding. But I am also glad that they are finally touching. Gwen needs it. As Gwen's crying subsides, they lean back together into the couch and continue watching the screen. No words are exchanged. I know everything has been said already. If not today, then before I ever came to be with Gwen. I see Robert's arm moving steadily back and forth and know he is rubbing her arm. As Gwen carefully wipes the wet mascara from under her eyes, the last thing I see is her perfect pink fingernail.

The orange light hits me like a nuclear blast. I couldn't have been more taken aback. The world disappears as the loud roar rises up around me and consumes me. As the darkness bears down upon me and pulls me away, I feel not only unprepared, but disappointed. I don't want to leave Gwen. But I don't have time to think about any more about her as the noise and chaos ends abruptly and I am greeted by the unlikely sight of a urinal.

9 TRYING

I am still reeling. The stark white porcelain swims in front of me and the stream of urine coming from some guy I am now visiting splashes down the drain. He turns quickly, seems to lose his balance a bit, and walks toward the sinks a little too quickly. Oh boy, I think, another professor-type walk I will have to get used to. He leans heavily on the counter and looks up into the mirror. He is broad and well-muscled; his biceps are big and straining to get out of his shirt. The second thing I notice about him are his eyes. Deep set and shadowed by a heavy brow ridge, they give him the look of a Neanderthal. The dark circles under his eyes probably make the effect more pronounced. He looks a bit rough, with a square jaw and a couple of scars visible on his forehead and chin. His nose is slightly red, as if he had just blown it. I suppose some women might find him ruggedly handsome, but I think he just looks like a thug. His broad and square shoulders are those of a linebacker, and his barrel chest could probably stop one. I hear water running to the left of me, and when my guy reaches for the soap dispenser, I am able to see the other man at the sink. He looks up briefly, and the two exchange nods. I watch as the guy I am in washes his hands, revealing dry, cracked skin that looks as if it might be a little painful to wash. After the other man leaves the restroom with the creak of a door, my guy looks at himself again in the mirror and, instead of drying his hands, turns on the water again and splashes some on his face. He does it quickly, making me dizzy as the big hands rub across my field of vision. He sighs and wipes his face dry with a paper towel.

The restaurant we are in has the look of an all-American chain restaurant, with faux Americana antiques lining shelves high up on the walls; bright, primary-colored table cloths, menus, and booth seats; and dishes of food heaped so high and wide they would easily exceed a grown man's recommended daily caloric intake. We walk through the restaurant back to a table. I want him to sit down as soon as possible. His walk might just be worse than the professor's—either that or I had really gotten used to Gwen's gait. He approaches a booth where a woman and two children look up at his approach. I can't say they exactly look glad to see him return.

The woman seems middle-aged, as I guess him to be, but has the look of someone who is actually much younger than her skin suggests. I consider myself an expert in this area. I can analyze a woman's face and body and guess her age to within a few years, whether she has had children, if she used sunscreen in her twenties, and whether she leads a stressful life. I used to make a game out of it with bartenders. We would wager, I would talk to a woman at the bar to get the information, and I would always win. This woman looks to be forty-five but is likely closer to thirty-eight, did not use sunscreen enough and maybe still doesn't, and is very stressed out. I can't see her hips and stomach, but it's a fair guess that the children at the table are hers.

She meets our eyes briefly and then grabs her water glass and takes a long drink. The kids also avoid his gaze and busy themselves with the tiny plastic swords that have come with their meals. I assume the two kids are his because both the boy and the girl have his deep-set eyes and brow ridge. Genetics are a bitch. He slides unsteadily into the booth, giving me vertigo that would have been enough to make me vomit, if I had the ability.

"How's that burger, Mike?" A booming voice emerges from the body I am in and startles me. I shouldn't be surprised that the linebacker has a powerful voice.

"Fine," the boy answers quietly while chewing. He glances at the girl meeting her eyes briefly. Something isn't being said, but I have missed it. Maybe they had a fight. I am not getting much yet in the way of emotion from my new host. I can feel a touch of anxiety, but it is muddled and hard for me to read.

"You ever tried ketch-aise?" the man now asks the boy with forced enthusiasm.

"Huh?" The boy stops chewing and looks skeptically at his dad.

"Ketchup and mayonnaise mixed together. It's the best thing to dip your fries into, trust me!" I can hear the smile in the man's voice and also a slight slurring of his words. The boy raises an eyebrow like he thinks his dad is crazy. Ah, another area of my extensive expertise: alcohol. This might explain the dizzy walk too. The linebacker looks around the room and his gaze stops on a waitress nearby.

"Excuse me!" He calls her much too loudly. The waitress hears him, even though she is three tables away.

"Dad!" The boy looks nervous.

"Trust me, Mike," the man replies, a little too quickly. She comes over quickly, looking nervous. "Can we get some mayo over here?" he asks.

"Yes, of course, I'll be right back." The waitress looks relieved at the simple request.

"Dad, I don't want to try it! Sounds gross!" Mike wails. The man doesn't say anything but looks at the woman across the table. She looks annoyed. He reaches for a tumbler in front of him that contains brown liquid and ice that is mostly melted. He drinks the rest of it down, ice and all.

"Marie, you'll try it, won't you?" He slurs the words and looks down at the little girl next to him on the bench seat. She is probably around five years old. She is the first one to smile at him.

"I'll try it, Dad! I don't think it will be gross," she says in what can only be described as a perfect Disney little-girl voice.

"That's my girl!" He pats her shoulder. It looks like a catcher's mitt swiping at a butterfly.

"Let's ask for our check when she brings the mayo," the woman says, speaking softly and evenly.

"Are we in a hurry, Diane? Marie and I want to enjoy our ketch-aise." He must have smiled at Marie again because she grins back when he looks at her. I catch Diane rolling her eyes when he looks past her again. She starts digging through her purse.

It's an awkward finish to the meal with Linebacker and Marie exclaiming over their fries and dip, while the boy and the woman watch silently. This guy's emotions are erratic—happy and childlike at times, angry and sullen at others. I chalk it up to the alcohol. He doesn't seem all that drunk to me. Buzzed definitely, but not drunk. But I get the feeling that's why the woman, presumably his wife, is angry.

I grasp his emotions even though they are an unsteady craft in a choppy ocean. I have come to rely on the emotions of my host. I realize that I almost crave them in order to have some experience of reality, something tangible, the only tangible aspect of my life now. Can I even call it life? I need to feel my host's emotions just so that I can *feel* something, anything. And after spending so much time with Gwen's muted emotions, I welcome anything the linebacker gives me, no matter how confusing it may be.

As the family walks to the car, I am able to see the license plate on their Ford F-250. The state is Montana, and the plates expire in September 2015. I am glad to get my bearings. I don't know how this soul traveling works, but it is somewhat of a comfort to know I am still in the same year. As soon as Diane gets into the driver's seat and starts the truck, I see her press a button on the dashboard, and I can hear a cartoon start to play somewhere behind me. My guy slouches in his seat and sticks his legs as far out as the area under the dashboard will allow.

"Put your seatbelt on, Dean," Diane says sharply. My host—Dean is his name—stares out the window for a moment, taking in the packed parking lot artificially lighting up the black evening. Then he slowly puts his belt on, without a glance at her or word uttered.

The drive is beautiful. I have never been to Montana; I never had any reason to go there. I'm not exactly an outdoorsy guy. But the rolling hills with sandstone peeking through the soil and geometric patches of grass are unlike anything I have seen before. The setting sun gives the land the look of a movie set. We drive for thirty minutes before we arrive at another town, smaller than the one we just left. Dean falls asleep, and I am in the dark for most of the ride. But I don't need to see to know that during this time no one in the car has spoken. The cartoons keep the kids quiet, and I'm sure that is intentional.

Their house is at the end of a long dirt road and

appears to be on a sizable piece of property. The place looks shabby and at least thirty years old. I miss my condo in Chicago. I miss the cool of the black tile on my feet in the kitchen and the shiny flecks of silver in the granite countertop. I remember how the balcony door creaks right before it closes, how the couch fits me perfectly when I sit on the left side and lean my elbow on the arm while watching TV. Why are these the things I remember? Shouldn't I have memories of the things I did there, you know, with people? I think about how solitary my life has been. I thought I wanted it that way. I have no complications, no drama, nothing tying me down. But if all that it leaves me is a warm and fuzzy feeling about my countertops, I'd say I'm not getting a whole lot out of life. I feel a pang of regret—a feeling that is unfamiliar to me. I've also never wanted children. Many a relationship of mine ended when the uterus-minded party found out this bit of information and acted as if I should have shared it on the first date. So as long as I'm regretting not having closer relationships, I might as well see if I'm missing anything by not having kids while visiting Dean. Although I have a feeling that this might not be a model family.

I can tell Dean has sobered up as he walks up the driveway. Once inside the house, he heads down a long, narrow flight of stairs into the basement. As we enter the low, dark basement I quickly recognize the space as what would be referred to as a man cave. I mentally shake my head in disgust at the thought of the American wife. She decorates the entire house with no reference to the man's tastes or preferences; sequesters him in the basement, garage, or workshop; and then complains to her friends that he spends too much time in his man cave. *What is he doing down there for all that time?* the wives wonder aloud to each other. He's jerking off to porn because you never give him any, that's what he's doing.

As I survey the room with its neon-beer-sign memorabilia, pool table, plasma screen, and wet bar, I quickly return to loving my single life—screw relationships. I have all this at my place, minus the wife. Well, I don't have a neon sign with Budweiser frogs repeatedly jumping onto a lily pad.

Dean switches on the TV, and ESPN fills the enormous screen. This is turning out to be one stereotype come to life after another. He makes a drink at the wet bar and grabs a bag of pretzels. By making a drink, I mean that he pours Crown Royal into a tumbler, no ice. When he opens the cabinet, I notice it is nearly bare, just the bottle of Crown and an ancient looking bottle of Kahlua, which every home bar seems to have. It's a pathetic bar for a man cave. He stops and stares at the glass in his hand before he drinks, swirling the contents around slowly, eyes fixed on but not really seeing it. I wait for an emotion to come through to me, as I am certain he is lost in thought. I feel nothing. It worries me that he isn't giving me anything. I learned a lot from being with Gwen. Then, snapping out of his trance, he raises the glass and takes a long drink, closing his eyes and sending me to darkness for a few seconds.

For the next hour or so, Dean and I watch a detailed debrief of the Daytona 500, which apparently has taken place earlier that day. I am held captive, and there is no escape. I'm trapped in white-trash hell. This couldn't be further from my life. I have never been a sports guy, a convenient trait that has worked to my advantage when trying to get a girl to go home with me. Once I tell a girl that I hate sports, she will sigh with relief, smile, and lean in closer to tell me how her ex-boyfriend wouldn't even pry himself off the couch on Sundays to screw her. That's when I tell her that I only use my couch *for* screwing. Depending on the girl, that either makes her eyes flash with desire, or it turns her off and leads to a "well, it was nice meeting you ending." It's best to weed out the ones that are so easily turned off early anyway. I want to see that flash of naughty before I proceed.

And so I am forced to listen and watch as film from the race is slowed down so that we can see how this guy's tire broke loose at a certain point and where the fender on the Ford hit the wall and other such bullshit. It makes me want to shoot myself. I obviously can't look away so I make a game out of counting the mullets I see in the crowd shots and interviews, and when I tire of that, I play "real or fake" with the groupie chicks in pit row after the race. My fun is ruined when I hear the door at the top of the stairs open and the sound of shoes on the unfinished wood stairs. I assume Diane is approaching but am not given the opportunity to look at her as Dean continues to stare straight ahead at the TV. I see her out of the corner of his eye as she sits down on the other side of the L-shaped couch. After a long, awkward silence, she speaks, and I feel Dean's world shift around him.

"I didn't know you had more of that shit down here. When did you buy it?" Her tone is accusatory and bitter. Dean finally turns his head and looks at her. As he does, his emotions slam into me. They are so strong that I feel sick. I feel it and know it well: anger. He studies her with narrowed eyes. She looks hard and cold. Her posture speaks of tension and a brace for a fight.

"Yesterday," he says, challenging her.

"You know, I thought we could have a nice dinner out as a family without you ruining it by getting drunk. We drove all the way over there, used the gas that truck guzzles, and then spent extra money on your drinks." She glares at him, her hands clasped together tightly.

"I can't have a few drinks with dinner? Christ, what are you, my mother?" He turns defiantly back to the TV. She stands up and walks in front of the screen.

"Don't be an ass. Why do we have to have this same conversation a million times? Why is it so hard? Why can't you stay in control for just a couple of hours? Has it gotten that bad?" Her last question has a hint of concern in it. I pick up on it, but I don't think he does. I feel rolls of anger boiling inside him.

"It just makes things easier," he says simply. His "fuck off" tone can't be more clear.

"Easier how?"

"Just easier." He is pushing her buttons and enjoying it. I feel a spring of pleasure well up within the hot mass of rage.

"Easier to be around me and the kids, you mean."

"Yeah." He doesn't even hesitate.

"Are we that hard to tolerate? Am I?" She doesn't look as if she is hearing this for the first time. No, this argument has the feel of one that has been rehearsed over and over again. The actors know their lines and stick to them. The play always remains the same, act after act, year after year.

"Sometimes," he answers, looking her square in the eye. "When I'm *not* drinking, you're worried about me drinking and watching my every move, waiting for me to screw up, telling your friends on the phone what a fuck-up I am, and piling on the chores like you're punishing me. When I am drinking, all that is much easier to handle because you stop talking to me and I can just...disappear." He trails off and stares down into his empty glass. She sits down again, and her shoulders slump in defeat. I did not expect her to give up this easily.

"Where do you go?" she asks quietly.

"What?"

"Where do you disappear to, in your mind?"

"Somewhere not here. Somewhere in another life."

"Why don't you go find another life, then?" Her

bitterness increases as his answer sets her off. I'm glad I'm not feeling her emotions; they are changing so unpredictably. "You can't stop drinking. You never will. You'll never be the man you once were. You know it, and I know it." Now she sounds like someone who is ready to fight again. And a fight she gets. In one swift motion, Dean throws his glass onto the concrete floor. She jumps up from the couch in surprise. He stands up slowly, and she looks small before him. I can feel him losing control, feel the frustration tangling with the anger in a twisted dance.

"I. Am. Trying!" he roars with the ferociousness of a taunted lion.

"Trying! Trying?" she scoffs. "*How* are you trying? You just told me that you drink on purpose to escape from me."

"Do you think I want to live like this? Do you think I want to end up like my dad? Hell no. But I don't know how to try harder, Diane. Don't you get it—this is in me. This *is* me, no matter how hard I try." Within the rage I now feel a touch of regret and sadness deep within him. I am continually amazed at how complex emotions can be. I'm learning to read them like a sommelier reads wine. I'm getting notes of a traumatic childhood here. And, hmm, let's see…yes, I detect resentment toward a parent. I would much rather have been tasting wine.

"Well it's been five years of trying. Five years of me being patient—" Diane begins.

"Patient?" he yells.

"Yes, going to therapy with you, lying about your DUIs to my friends, and cleaning up your vomit! I'm done with you *trying*."

"You're not fucking listening! I don't know how to fight this anymore. I've tried everything. Do you ever think that maybe some people just can't be cured of this, Diane?"

"Thousands are, all the time! What's so special about you?" she sneers. Instead of replying, he strides over to the bar, grabs a new glass, and fills it with ice. His hands are shaking, and his vision is slightly blurred.

"Don't you fucking do it! You've had enough! You aren't a man; a man knows when to stop." Her words punch through the air like machine gun bullets. His emotions are running so high that I think the shaking hands and blurred vision are from anger, not alcohol. I am sure he will turn to strike her at any moment.

But I am wrong about that. He stops, sets the glass down, and braces himself with both hands against the countertop. He leans down until his head is hanging between his arms, and I can hear him taking big gulps of air. Through the anger comes another emotion. It is tough to pinpoint at first. I struggle with it, but as it grows stronger and overtakes the anger, I recognize it. It is shame. He has his eyes closed, and without sight I feel his inner self even more strongly. Shame, insecurity, and weakness run together and create a multidimensional feeling. He is so broken inside that I wish I could show Diane what he is feeling. There is no doubt that she would be changed forever if she could experience it, if she knew the truth. I know in an instant that he is not the tough guy he appears to be. For him, I realize, shame equals hopelessness. He sees no way out and that only serves to increase his shame at his weakness.

Dean's eyes open suddenly, and I see why. Diane has come around the bar, and I see her hand resting on his arm. She starts to say something, but I can't hear it. I am being taken away again. I hear the roar build around me and feel a strong and unrelenting pull. There is something about her hand that I won't forget: her diamond wedding ring glinting in the light. A relic of the past that refuses to dim. Its reflective surface metaphorically shows all their flaws and all the hurt that they have created between them. I will never know if her hand on him is to physically stop him or if it represents comfort and acceptance. For some reason this really bothers me. But why I care is beyond me. *What is happening to me?*

10 HUMBLE

Fire and smoke. When I arrive in my new host, the first thing I see is gray smoke swirling in front of an orange glow. I am so startled that I try to turn and run, just out of instinct. When that fails, of course, I try to adjust. But my view is obscured and I want to rub my eyes and blink hard. I am in a hallway that is most likely in someone's home, given the family photos hanging on the walls. The fire is up ahead, but I can't tell how bad it is because the smoke is so thick. I'm alarmed that the person I'm in doesn't seem to be moving away from the fire but instead is walking toward it. Did they start the fire? Are they trapped? The thoughts fill my head and I search the scene for any clues I can gather.

My new body seems shorter than the linebacker's and I'm glad to find that whoever it is has a normal and steady gait. I catch a glimpse of a hand and notice the thick black glove, covered at the wrist by the sleeves of a thick tan coat with yellow stripes near the cuff. A spark of recognition fires in me and I realize that it's a fireman's coat. We proceed down the hallway and I hear a chilling "chhooo-cheeee" of breath coming through a mask. My panic slightly subsides at the knowledge that I'm in a highly trained professional. But still, this highly trained professional will walk willingly right into that smoke and fire and we may not walk back out.

We walk swiftly and calmly, heading into a room on the right. The gloved right hand reaches out and runs along the door while pushing it all the way open. It is dark inside the room.

"Door!" A strong male voice booms in my head, startling me. He enters the room and raises his hand to switch on a headlamp. He moves to the right, running his hand along the wall.

"Penny?" he yells out into the hazy air. "I'm a firefighter. Remember us from school? Don't be afraid. Where are you?" He speaks calmly and reassuringly as he continues to sweep the room. He approaches a child's twin bed and lowers to one knee beside it. I see him bring a long bar in front of him, which he passes under the bed, feeling for any resistance of the human sort, I assume. He pulls it back and stands again. *Chhooo-cheeee, chhooo-cheeee, chhooo-cheeee*, the eerie breathing noise punctuates the tense scene. He finishes his circuit of the room by looking in the small closet. "Penny?"

The man's emotions abruptly slam into me. They are possibly the strongest feelings I have felt yet from a host. There is no mistaking what I am sensing. It is pure and undeniable determination with big doses of worry and stress. I would guess that his determination comes from knowing he is really skilled at something and that nothing will make him doubt himself. But I know his stress is related to the girl he is searching for. I keep thinking about that orange glow at the end of the hallway.

"Attack Two to command, I have cleared the first bedroom," he says loud and clear as he reenters the hall. Now I can see a coiled fire hose on the floor, snaking out through an open window at this end of the hallway. I glimpse the top of a ladder leaning against the house. Another voice comes through what must be a headset, crackling and distant.

"Copy. First bedroom clear."

We move to the right across the hall into another bedroom that is also dark but seems free of fire. Hazy gray smoke hangs like a heavy fog. *Chhooo-cheeee, chhooo-cheeee.*

It's another kid's room; I can see a Disney rug on the floor.

"Door!" he says into the radio. It's a repeat of what we did in the first room, moving to the right, always touching the wall with our right hand. Closet cleared, underneath bed cleared. "Penny! Where are you? Please yell out and let me know where you are! I'm a firefighter, don't be scared." Despite his words, I feel worry and concern rise in him when there is still no answer. "Attack Two to command, I have cleared the second bedroom."

"Copy. Second bedroom clear," comes the voice in the headset.

"Attack One to command, lower section stairs cleared," says a different male voice in the headset. As we walk down the hallway, getting closer to the orange glow, I can faintly hear voices and noises coming from the lower level of the house. We pass by an open balcony that would probably afford a view into the lower living area if it weren't obscured by smoke. We proceed to another doorway. The smoke is so thick now that the room beyond doesn't come into view until we step through the doorway. The orange glow is much brighter and closer.

"Door!" He announces another room. This bedroom is so filled with smoke that a hand upon the wall is absolutely necessary. The fire burning at the opposite side of the room appears to stretch from the floor to the ceiling. I feel my host's determination increase. It's so focused and clear that I feel like I know exactly what to do in this situation. I feel complete confidence in what he is doing. But I'm also scared shitless.

As he circles the perimeter of the room, he comes close to a window that lets enough daylight in for me to see a dresser with jewelry and purses on it. This one is an adult bedroom, and as we move around the room, I can tell it is three times bigger than the other bedrooms. I become even more alarmed as we near the fire and I can see that the bed is ablaze, along with the nightstand, the carpet in some areas, and the ceiling. There is another door in the bedroom, which is open, and fire is bursting out from it and running up the wall to the ceiling like a reverse waterfall. I can see tile flooring in that next room and figure it's an adjoining bathroom.

"Penny!" he calls with more urgency now. *Chhoo-chee*; his breathing is faster now. "Penny, where are you?"

I am captivated by the fire and the psychedelic swirling smoke. I have never seen anything like it. Thankfully, the firefighter doesn't stand and stare as I would have. He uses the long bar to sweep under the bed to no avail. The fire snaps and cracks nearby.

"Attack One to command, upper section stairs cleared. Moving to room of origin," a voice sounds in the headset, and I can hear the thumping of nearby footsteps along with some other unidentifiable noises. Just then the bed crashes to the floor unevenly, one of its legs giving out. No longer captivated, I am filled with an intense desire for flight. Yet, here I am, trapped inside the body of a man who will fight on.

As he moves around the bed to the opposite wall, the smoke seems determined to blind us. Hand on the wall, he drops to his knees and begins to crawl. The fire is behind us, now, and to our right. I feel his concern begin to outweigh his anxiety but that only seems to heighten his resolve. His feelings are so incredibly strong that I take them on as my own. I need to find this child. The man's gaze stops on the edge of a small door in the lower part of the wall next to us. It's about three feet tall and has a small brass knob on it. A small storage door—bingo.

"Penny!" After he yells I think I can hear a sound coming from behind the door. I feel hope rise up in him. He pulls on the door, but it doesn't budge. The second time he put more strength into it and yanks it open so forcefully that the top hinge breaks loose. He leans in and his headlamp illuminates a terrified face in the darkness. A little girl, she's maybe three years old, with red hair clinging to her tearstained face. Her eyes are squinted closed in distress. Her little cheeks are red and perspiration drips down her temples. I know it must be hot in that storage area, but I am relieved to see it is free of smoke or fire. Intense relief and happiness also floods through my host.

"Penny, it's OK, honey. I'm here to help you. I'm a firefighter. I'm going to take you to your mom, OK?" She stops crying and stares at him with big eyes but makes no motion to come toward him. "Attack Two to command, I have located the female child. She's conscious and uninjured."

"Copy Attack Two. You may descend via cleared stairs."

He reaches in and holds out his gloved hands to her. Smoke is swirling in around her now.

"My name is Ken. Like Barbie and Ken, right?" She nods a little at this and coughs. "I'm going to pick you up now." As he puts his hands around her torso she finally leans in and crawls forward to him. He brings her to his chest in a swift movement. There is another loud crash from the room, and the girl flinches in his arms and starts to scream.

"You are so brave, Penny!" he says, his voice filled with elation despite the nearby chaos. I am still terrified. "Close your eyes, sweetie," he instructs. He crawls on knees and one arm, while holding her to him with his other arm. The smoke is filling the room and only about three feet near the floor is free of it. We head toward the bedroom door. I think I can hear the sound of high-pressure water. I hope that's what it is.

We half crawl, half crouch down the hallway toward the stairs. The smoke ceiling is higher now. Two other firefighters outside a door directly across from the stairs are controlling a fire hose and directing water into the room. The orange glow is fading quickly. Ken stands up almost fully and heads toward the stairs. The firefighters exchange a quick look before Ken descends. I feel elation well up inside him.

"Attack Two to command, descending stairs with female child."

"Copy Attack Two," comes the immediate reply. I can feel the joy surging through him and wonder if he is actually smiling. He must have adrenaline pumping through him, and I wonder how that transfers to emotions and what I can feel.

He strides upright through the lower level, which is free of smoke. He shifts Penny so she is sitting on his forearm and leaning into him. She continues to wail and shake. We come out the open front door, and I can hear the shrieks of a woman close by, repeatedly calling the girl's name. I feel Ken flood with relief, as if the woman's voice relieves him of his last bit of anxiety.

The next few minutes are a blur of activity. Fortunately, I can see more now because Ken removes his mask and helmet. He pulls off his thick gloves and wipes his eyes. Penny has been placed into the distraught woman's arms, and she is kissing the little girl's face and trying to calm her down. The woman and child have the same red hair and the woman holds her with the intensity of a mother. Paramedics appear with oxygen, ready to look Penny over. Reluctantly, the woman hands her over and turns to Ken. She catches him in a fierce hug and gives possibly the most heartfelt thank-you I have ever heard in my life. Ken is filled with happiness, and with a sense of accomplishment. But after the embrace, he seems to want to move along and get out of the center of attention. He stammers his humble replies as the woman continues to talk to him and others look on in admiration. He checks in with the other ground crew and hears that the fire has been put out. A candle in the bathroom had ignited the shower curtain.

Ken looks around the yard and street. People are lining up along the sidewalk; police, ambulance, and news crews announce their presence through silently flashing colored lights. He heads for the fire truck and grabs a water bottle out of a built-in cooler on the side. I can see that people are looking at him. I feel embarrassment in him and surmise it's from all the attention. He turns his back to the crowd. But as he drinks the entire bottle of water in one long swallow, I can feel that sense of accomplishment outweighing everything else. He feels good about what he has done but doesn't come across as cocky. I get the impression that he has done this many times before, that he sees it as a job to be done, and that it only has one possible outcome in his mind.

An overeager young reporter from the local news makes her way to Ken before he can escape into the truck. He quickly utters a few responses about not being a hero and how happy he was to see Penny in her mother's arms, then escapes as soon as he can. I do however discover my current whereabouts. The reporter's microphone base bears the station handle logo, as well as the word "Denver." I am excited to find out where I am so quickly after joining a host. I used to visit Denver on business and always enjoyed the area.

Ken helps the other firefighters recoil the hoses and put away all the equipment. When they are finished with their job and the crowd has died down, he walks into the front yard and leans down to run his hands over the ground. His eyes roam over the dirt and grass and rest upon a small rock. He pulls it out and brushes the caked dirt off; it is smooth and gray with white flecks. Ken examines it closely. Satisfied, he straightens up. I can't see it, but I think he puts the rock in a pocket of his bulky coat. He glances around to see if anyone is looking, then walks to the truck and climbs up into a seat.

~

I drink in the surroundings as we ride in the fire truck back to the station. Distant mountains stretch for miles along the horizon. It's clearly summertime, most likely late summer, maybe August: the leaves on the trees have that dull green look they get from being out in the weather for months. The lawns are turning brown. And the kiddie pools in the front lawns are half-filled with dirty water as if the children have tired of them by summer's end. My perceptions are getting better each time I visit someone. When you have no sense of smell, taste, or touch, and when you are dropped into a landscape without any information, you have to rely on other clues. This *looks* like August. The earth looks heated and worn from a long, hot summer, as if it has finished browning in the toaster and is about to come out into the cool air. July would have a different look, I think. As would June. And each season has its own associations. When I was a kid, the things I loved about summer were baseball, drinking from the garden hose, water-balloon fights, and staying outside until well after dark.

Now I associate summer with women, skin, sundresses, and bikinis. I am so starved for those that I find myself searching the streets for women in their summer garb. It feels a little pathetic. Regardless, I am hoping that Ken is as straight as an arrow. Because, being a firefighter, he is sure to get some decent ass on a regular basis. And maybe I will get to stick around to witness that. OK, yes, it is pathetic.

~

Ken and I spend the remainder of the afternoon at the station filling out paperwork and discussing the fire with the Fire Chief. We shoot hoops with the other guys right after the shift ends, which proves to be the biggest test of my vertigo yet. But after a while, I find that I can anticipate Ken's next move as he plays as I would. Slowly I begin to feel one with him, and it shocks the hell out of me. I had been with the others for longer without feeling as if I were a part of them. But something is happening with Ken that hadn't happened with the others. I feel more real. I feel more alive. When he dribbles the ball, runs, and jumps to complete a layup, I can almost feel us come off the ground. Almost. Since I don't have the other senses to rely on, it actually just appears to me that I am floating through the air. It is exhilarating, and I don't want the game to stop.

The guys give Ken a hard time for only playing ball for about ten minutes, but he tells them he is beat and just wants to go. On the road, his beat up Buick makes almost more noise than a fire engine. It has seen better days. As we drive by several restaurants and bars I will him to pull over. I feel like a little kid begging to stop for ice cream. *Oh plllleeeeeeasssse, please, can we stop? Let's go have some fun. I need to see women dressed up and flirting. I need to see the sly looks across the room, as people picture each other naked. C'mon, Ken, we can get you laid tonight.*

But, he drives on. We are going home, I assume. A new home, another home, another life. Although I am disappointed, a part of me is anxious to see how yet another person chooses to live. It is as if I am filming a documentary, except I am a director without any control over how the film will play out.

He doesn't live too far from the station, so I don't get to see much of the area. Plus, I have never really realized how much you miss when you drive. Because your attention is focused directly ahead of you, most of the landscape is out of sight. As a result, I don't get to see much except roads and cars and commercial buildings flanking the road. He pulls into a neighborhood that could best be described in two words: unimaginative suburbs. I can imagine the developers saying, "Just leave enough room between the houses for a skinny dog to slink through and use the same floor plan for all the houses so we don't have to think much as we build them." Ken pulls into a garage that is devoid of any bikes, trikes, balls, water guns, or big wheels. No kids? I like it. Bachelor? Bachelor firefighter getting a lot of ass? Not so fast—from my limited view I can see a two-door Honda parked in the garage. *A chick car,* I think. Ken grabs a beer from the fridge by the door to the house, and I berate him for being so boring. *We could have done that in a much more interesting venue, buddy.*

The kitchen is an homage to Elvis Presley. All of the décor is centered around him: Elvis trays on the wall, an Elvis toaster, an Elvis spoon rest, Elvis fridge magnets, and an Elvis clock whose disjointed lower body looks as if it probably swings from side to side on the hour. My thoughts are interrupted by a female voice.

"Hey there, husband." The female voice is soft and sweet. Ken responds automatically.

"What's up, wife?" He sounds contented, as if repeating a favorite quote. His inner emotions match the sound of his voice, and I feel his happiness. He turns to face a petite woman with blond hair cut in a pixie style—she's cute in a Tinkerbell sort of way. She smiles warmly at him and they come together in an embrace. It's so different from Gwen and Robert that I am taken aback by the ease of their affection. I feel a new emotion spread through him, and everything just seems to slow down and ease up as any remaining tension from today's ordeal melts away. It's an interesting feeling and very welcoming after my experiences with the last two people I have visited. He is at least a foot taller than she is, and he buries his face in her hair and closes his eyes. When he pulls back and looks into her eyes it hits me—I feel *love*. Yet, how do I know it is love? I've never been in love. But Ken is radiating joy, contentment, protectiveness and pure happiness all at the same time. I believe that these must be love's main ingredients.

"Soooo, just a regular ol' day at the office, right? Nothing special?" she says with there's laughter in her voice. He pulls back; she is smiling. I'm sure he is too.

"Yeah. Nothing exciting. Just the usual," he says. He lets his hands move to her waist, still holding her close. Her face gets more serious.

"I heard about the woman and the girl," she says softly, her blue eyes searching his.

"And there was a dog too," Ken says.

"There's always a dog," she says with a little smile. Ken chuckles and gently breaks the embrace. But I see her hand shoot out, and she must have grabbed his hand again because he stops and looks at her.

"Seriously. Are you OK?" She asks the question softly. There's a meaning behind her eyes that is just for them. I would think firefighters have conversations like this with their spouses often, with one of them perpetually worried.

"I'm OK," Ken answers. But his emotions can't lie. I feel unease come over him, and an unsettled feeling. It is a quick change from his emotions just moments earlier. I don't remember ever being this emotionally fluid in life. Do only complicated people switch from one emotion to the next so quickly? I thought it was only hormonal women. Or perhaps I do it too and just never realized it because I didn't have the perspective I have now.

The woman continues to look into his eyes. "I'm proud of you. Every time. Even though I'm crazy-scared, I'm proud," she says. They look at each other a moment longer, and then he reaches down to brush a quick kiss against her lips.

"Now, what did you make me for dinner, woman?" he says with a laugh in his voice as he walks farther into the kitchen. I can almost feel him trying to push the unease inside of him away.

"Well, I'm a total loser wife and didn't make anything because I got home from work late and have spin class in twenty minutes," she explains as she pulls open the fridge door and grabs an Elvis water bottle.

"A man could starve around here," Ken grumbles as he reaches for some sandwich bread on the counter. I can feel him smile though. I'm getting good at this.

~

Ten minutes later Ken's wife is heading for the door as he is eating his sandwich and chips at the coffee table in front of the TV while *The Simpsons* play out their antics on the screen. She stops halfway through the doorway and turns to look at him. He looks away from the screen.

"Did you get one for the dog?" she asks in a somber tone. Ken stares at her for several beats and then puts his sandwich down on the plate and leans back on the couch. There is a weight to this particular question that I don't understand.

"No," Ken pauses. "He was already downstairs. Doesn't count."

She gives a half smile and a little nod.

"I love you. Eat some fruit," she says as she leaves.

"I love you too."

As we sit here eating and watching TV, I feel the unease creeping into him again. I also feel melancholy mixed in. I chalk it up to his hellish day. Anyone would feel uneasy after a day like that. I'm surprised he's functioning as normally as he is. But he doesn't laugh at the *The Simpsons* and begins to stare out the window at the small backyard. I can see an Elvis rain gauge attached to the deck railing. Ken continues to stare, lost in thoughts I can only feel, for several minutes. When he rises suddenly from the couch, I feel a wave of dizziness. He switches the TV off and walks very slowly to the fireplace at the far end of the room. He approaches the mantle, which is bare except for an ornate pair of ceramic candlesticks at either side and a large hand-carved wooden box right in the center. He stops in front of the box and looks down at his hands. The smooth gray rock he had picked up earlier is there; I don't know how long he has been holding it. He turns it over and over in his hand, his thumb feeling its smooth shape.

Suddenly, without warning, sorrow ambushes me. The switch is quick. It is as if sorrow has been wearing the costume of unease. But it hits Ken, and therefore me, hard. I didn't know before now that sadness and sorrow feel very different. To be sad is one thing, but what I feel right now comes from the depths of the soul. It's different than Professor Trenholm's heartbreak. It feels deep-rooted in something more serious. I can't explain how I know this. I hear Ken take a sharp breath, as if he is as surprised as I am in his shift of emotions. His fist closes around the rock but not before I see his vision get watery and a splash of a tear hit his hand. Sorrowful pain explodes in us then, sorrow so deep that I think I feel a touch of tangible pain. But I can't focus on the feeling and it slips away, or was never actually there. He gasps again and struggles to even out his breathing, forcing himself to move air steadily out his mouth. He raises his head and his hands, and his free hand flips open the brass latch on the wooden box in front of him. He eases the lid open until it rests against the back of the mantle. The box is half full of rocks, twenty or thirty of them, of different sizes, shapes, and colors. But each would fit easily in the palm of a man's hand. Ken hesitates and then slowly and carefully places the rock he picked up that day on top of the pile in the box, picking a spot for it. Time slows to a stop as Ken whispers, "One for you, Bug," and closes the lid of the box. Tears are streaming from his eyes now.

As he slowly draws back from the fireplace, his eyes rest on a photograph hanging over the mantle. It's a young girl, about five years old or so. She resembles Ken's wife. She is standing on the lower half of a fence rail, leaning over, with her hand outstretched toward a horse that is only partially in the photo. Her head is turned toward the photographer, and a huge grin lights her face, showing the wonder of a young child's world. I finally realize that his sorrow has a more specific name and origin: it is grief. It consumes me now, and I am pulled down with him. It hurts like it had happened to me. All I know is that this is something I have never felt before, and I want to climb out of it.

I hear Ken control his breathing again, and he turns and walks away, wiping his eyes. Down the hallway he shuffles like a zombie, goes into a bedroom, and collapses on the bed fully clothed. His grief does not abate, but only seems to throb around me. Granted some mercy, he falls asleep quickly. He leaves me there, in the dark, hurting too.

11 SWITCH

I leave Ken in the night, but not before feeling his tormented mind disturb his sleep. I hear him mumbling words I can't quite understand and feel the emotions that dominate his nightmares: sorrow, anger, and fear, a combination that would torture anyone and so much more than I had felt with the professor. This is the depths of the human soul struggling to survive and stay sane. I don't want to leave Ken. Not in that state. But what can I do for him? He can't even feel my presence. They never can. As I am pulled away from him, I wonder if what I witnessed in that brief amount of time was exactly what I was supposed to experience. Obviously I'm not helping these people in any way so, are they helping me? Is this some sort of ghosts of Christmas past thing where some kooky angel is teaching me life lessons through each person I visit? Am I on my way to heaven, and are these stops along the way to make me think about my life? Well, it is certainly making me think about my life. My life is starting to stand out in stark comparison to the lives I have been witness to on this journey. I find myself feeling humbled at the range of emotions I never allowed my brain to let through in my own life. But where is the angel? He could at least appear every once in a while and give me an ETA.

The truth is, I can only hope this is the case.

~

When my sight returns, I see a large, colorful tower leaning over me. I am startled at first, until I realize the tower is made of wooden blocks, and judging by the small hand reaching out in front of me, I am probably about three feet tall. I am in a child. I watch as the hands steadily stack block after block on top of each other until the tower is swaying slightly. Then the hands stop, mid-stack, and freeze in midair. I hear a slight gasp from my new host. The child looks around quickly, and I see a small living room, sunlight streaming through windows, and blocks strewn all over the floor. The child is alarmed by something, but we are alone in the room. Slowly the child's gaze returns to the tower, and the hands stack another block on the top. Once again, we look around the room. We are still alone. When my view comes back around to the tower, the hand stacks one more block, and I watch as the tower falls in what seems like slow motion. The child remains silent and watches too.

We go on like this for a while, rebuilding the tower only to watch it fall again. It is oddly calming. I can hear kitchen sounds from nearby: pots being moved on the stove, the microwave running in short bursts, the faucet running, and a refrigerator door opening and closing. These are the sounds of a meal being prepared. Then light footsteps pad across the floor and adult feet in socks stand next to us.

"Dylan, dinner is ready." It's a man's voice. He

sounds pleasant.

"OK." The child's voice is from my host. Before he heads for the kitchen, his little hands reach down and scoop all the strewn blocks together and push them into a neat pile on the floor. A tottering and dizzying walk takes us on our way. Dylan heads toward the kitchen, but from the spinning sensation, he might as well be doing cartwheels.

"Hot dogs?" the small voice asks hopefully, looking up into a face that I assume is his father's. The man has brown hair cut in an ordinary and boring way, brown eyes, and a slightly chubby face. His smile is crooked and makes him look goofy.

"No hot dogs tonight, buddy. I made spaghetti and meatballs." The man guides the boy to the table with a motion of his hand.

"Awwww." Dylan makes the standard toddler sound of displeasure. The dad must have lifted him up from behind, because we suddenly seem to float up to the booster seat on a cheap wooden chair at the dining table. Dylan immediately puts his hands around the sippy cup already set at his place. I see Buzz Lightyear coming at me as the child lifts the cup to take a drink. He looks out the window close to him, and I can see enough to know we are in an apartment building. There is a railing directly outside, and I can see the other end of the L shape of the balcony curving around to the left and the doors to other apartments. After that my view is mostly limited to the food in front of me for the rest of the meal. The kid has an appetite. He is also quite smart. Even though I don't know his age, his vocabulary exceeds the cartoon characters on his divider plate. His dad talks to him throughout the meal, asking questions, playing word games, and making him laugh.

When the dad is cleaning the table at the end of the meal, Dylan asks, "Dad, is someone here when I play blocks?" His voice goes up in pitch at the end in genuine puzzlement.

"What, buddy? You want someone to play blocks with you?" the dad asks distractedly while he runs the water at the sink.

"Someone here...before?" Dylan tries again.

"Was someone here before? No, just me, bud. Why?"

"I don't know!" he says cheerily, waving his arms in front of him. "Down, Dad!" Once again we float up into the air and then down to the ground, and I feel the familiar vertigo. Dylan runs into the living room, returns to the pile of blocks, and this time starts making a house. He has been working on it for maybe five minutes when he suddenly freezes as he had done earlier, hand in midair, still as stone. He stands up and spins around so quickly, it takes me a few seconds to focus on what he can see. He is looking around the small living room and down the hallway that leads to the back of the apartment. I can't see what has grabbed his attention.

"Dad!" he yells. I hear footsteps running down the hallway and the man appears, looking alarmed.

"What's wrong?"

"Who is it?" Dylan asks. I can hear the alarm in his voice.

"Who is what?"

"Who is here, Dad?" The man hesitates and looks more concerned.

"What do you mean, bud? Did you hear something?"

"I...don't know. I...a man is here, I think," Dylan says and continues to look around the room, his gaze flickering into corners. The man strides to the sliding glass door at the side of the living room and pushes aside the blinds. I expect to see someone standing on the other side, but there is no one, just a small, sunny balcony off the back of the apartment. The dad then goes to the front door, and I hear him opening at least two locks and then the door. The boy stands rooted to the spot, listening. I can hear his dad's footsteps on the shared balcony and the sound of cars on a street. Soon his dad shuts the door and I hear the locks again.

"I don't see anyone, Dylan; everything's OK!" he says, coming back into the living room. He comes over to the boy and leans down to look him in the eye. "OK?" he asks.

The boy pauses. "OK, Dad." But he doesn't sound convinced.

~

The evening passes uneventfully. I lie on the living room floor with Dylan and watch *The Lion King*. I guess it could be worse. Could be better, though. Is he old enough to watch HBO?

The boy seems well behaved. Apart from a particularly whiny episode just before bedtime, he is remarkably calm and obedient. After the good-nights are said, the night-light comes on, and the dad closes the door, we lay in bed in the small room and stare at the glow-in-the-dark stars affixed to the ceiling. Then Dylan sits up slowly and looks around.

"Where are you?" he whispers, and I can hear the slight fear in his voice. "I don't see you." He stares at nothing for a while and then gets up to turn on the small lamp by the bed. "You here?" he asks again, a little less afraid now.

I have to admit, I am freaked out. This is like a scene out of a horror movie. I am half expecting a dark figure of a man or a demon or a ghost to materialize in front of us. I keep looking, right along with the boy, into every available space in front of us. But soon he turns off the lamp and gets back into bed, as if nothing has happened. He falls asleep surprisingly quickly for someone who had been so scared just minutes before. As I wait in the darkness and think about the recent changes in hosts, something that I can't quite pinpoint nags at me. I think about Ken and Gwen and wonder how they are doing. Then it comes to me, and I feel stupid that I haven't picked up on it yet. I don't *feel* Dylan's fear, it has just been implied. I haven't felt a thing from Dylan since I joined him. Not one single emotion, or even an undercurrent. I understood the reason for this in Gwen, but I would think that emotions would be raw and unfiltered in a small child. I wonder why I can't feel anything from this boy.

~

Dylan hums to himself while brushing his teeth. He brushes slowly, as if he has all the time in the world, despite the fact that his dad has just popped his head into the bathroom moments earlier to tell him to hurry up or he would be late to work. I am able to study the boy in the mirror as he stares into his mouth and brushes. He is a skinny little kid with thin, straight, brown hair that clings to his head. He has earnest eyes that make him seem too serious or perhaps wise beyond his years. I take in his facial features. I have learned in my journeys that doing so gives me a deeper tie to the person's emotions. It bothers me when I don't get to see the face of the person I am visiting, so when I have the opportunity like this, I drink it in. I wait to feel something from him, but there is just emptiness. It makes me extremely uneasy. After the boy is done, and his dad yells from the front of the apartment for the fourth time, he hops off a stool, stretches up to turn off the light, but then stops right in the doorway. He turns slowly back to the bathroom and turns on the light again. He peers over the counter into the mirror and whispers, "Are you in there?"

Understanding and disbelief hit me. Should I feel excited? This could be my first real connection to the world and to someone who senses my presence. My thoughts race, and I wonder if there is a way I can communicate with him. Maybe something got switched, and things are backward now. If that is the case, maybe he can feel *my* emotions…it is worth a try.

"Dylan, for God's sake!" The dad bellows from the hall and I hear him approaching fast.

"Coming! I'm coming." Dylan turns and runs down the hall.

~

In the car, from our vantage point from the backseat, I take in an urban area with no remarkable features. A lot of the time Dylan has his eyes in front of him while he plays with his Buzz Lightyear toy. His dad wears slacks and a button-down shirt that is frayed at the cuffs. I can only imagine how bad his shoes must be. He seems extremely stressed out, checking his phone at stoplights, and I recognize the look of corporate America. God, I miss that. I miss my iPhone. I miss my Armani suits. I miss the women that the Armani suits bring me. I miss the stress and the urgency of my life.

I return my focus to Dylan and our predicament. I decide to try my first experiment. I focus on the feeling of longing. It's an easy one to convey. I long to go back to my life. I long for things to be normal. I long for things to be different. I try to feel the emotion deeply and sincerely. I don't have to wait long before I get a reaction. Dylan blurts out, "Dad, why is he here?" He sounds curious more than anything else. And maybe just a little uneasy.

"Who?" The dad asks, still distracted.

"The man."

"Dylan, I don't know what you mean. What man?"

"The man! The man here with me." Dylan says with the exasperation of a child who can't understand why the adult isn't keeping up. "He's here again, and...I don't know why!" His voice rises an octave, and he raises his hands in front of him in a funny questioning gesture. I see his dad look at him in the rearview mirror, eyes narrowed with concern and confusion. Dylan looks down at the doll and starts picking at a loose plastic part.

"Do you have an imaginary friend, Dylan?" The dad sounds hopeful. Obviously, this would abate his worries. Too bad it isn't going to be as simple as that.

"What's...imma-gen-ary?" Dylan asks.

"It's an invisible friend that you make up. Only they aren't invisible to you, just to everyone else. It's someone nice for you to talk to and play with when no one else is around to play with," the dad says cheerily. Poor guy—this isn't going to go well.

"No...I don't see him." Dylan looks in vain around the backseat of the car and down around the floorboards.

"Oh. Then how do you know he's here?"

"He's just here, Dad! He's...up here." I see Dylan drop the action figure and raise both of his hands to his head. A couple of small chubby fingers partly cover our vision. The dad watches in the mirror again. His phone dings annoyingly beside him: new e-mails coming in.

"OK, buddy. Well, maybe you will make up what he looks like soon, and then you will see him, huh?" He turns into a parking lot and parks the car. Dylan is silent as his dad opens the car door and unfastens him from his car seat.

"Dad?"

"Uh-huh?"

"I think he might be mean." Dylan looks up into his dad's eyes as he is lifted from the car. The dad holds him in his arms and stares back. Worry flickers through the stress in his eyes. But before he can respond, another little boy calls to Dylan, excitedly telling him about the new toy he got.

"Dad, put me down! Hi, Devon!" Dylan yells over his dad's shoulder.

~

Dylan spends the day at day care, and I don't try my experiment again while he is there. I try my best to just observe and feel nothing about what I see. It must work because he doesn't say anything about me to anyone that day. The day is filled with finger painting, reading, sandbox playing, and enough yelling and screaming to provide emotional birth control for ten men. But I don't think too much about any of that. I am more consumed with why, of all the adjectives in the English language, this little boy described me as...mean.

~

My day is hellish. Forget fire and brimstone. My personal hell is a day-care center. Correction. My personal hell is a day-care center as seen from the eyes of a toddler, trapped and forced to endure it as an adult. Compared to the other kids, Dylan is a saint. He doesn't scream and whine when he doesn't get his way. He doesn't pick his nose. He doesn't have an annoying voice. Aside from crying and panicking when he cuts his leg on the slide, I'd say he is a pretty tolerable kid. But the other kids...no wonder their parents had looked so relieved when they dropped them off. I had assumed that they were rushing away to get to work on time, but after what I have witnessed, I figure they were probably just anxious to enjoy a quiet drive and a visit to Starbucks.

Dylan is more quiet and pensive than the other kids. It makes me wonder if he is always like this or if my presence is affecting him. If he is acting out of the ordinary today, the day-care workers don't say anything about it.

When his dad picks him up that afternoon, Dylan runs to him and throws his arms around his legs. I feel the same level of elation. Get me out of here. If I have to hear that Sasha girl screech one more time, I'm going to explode.

~

The evening is uneventful. Dylan watches TV, plays with his blocks, takes a bath, and pretends to read a couple of books while his dad listens. I notice his dad spends much of the evening on his laptop at the kitchen table. Ever patient, he lets Dylan interrupt him as often as needed and hardly shows a hint of impatience. He seems to feel guilty for working and tries to make up for it in little ways, like making jokes.

As usual, when my host lays down to sleep and the night sets in, I start to feel melancholy wash over me. I can't help the feelings of despair that creep in; I am beginning to think there is no end to my situation. How long will this cycle continue? I look into the eternal blackness and want to sleep too. I miss being unconscious for one-third of the day. I miss dreaming.

Suddenly Dylan's eyes open, and I can tell he is sitting up in bed. I can see the room, lit dimly by the night-light; everything seems normal. Dammit, he can feel me again.

"What you want?" Dylan asks, almost defiantly. I try answering him.

Nothing. I'm not supposed to be here, but I won't hurt you.

"I don't know you. You're...a stranger," Dylan says the last word in a whisper.

My name is Cole. I won't hurt you. Can you hear me? I ask the question with hope, but the boy sits silently, staring at the cartoon figures on his comforter. If I could have held my breath, I would have. But Dylan doesn't respond, he just lies back down and stares at the ceiling.

Please, can you hear me? Say yes if you can hear me. I try again. I want so badly for this to happen. It would mean so much to me. It's not like it would help me in any way. I just need the connection. I just need someone to know that I still exist. I haven't vanished. I'm still here, though no one knows. It's like being a prisoner on an island that no one knows about, an island that doesn't appear on any map.

But he says nothing. And what little hope I have left drifts away from my island like a leaf in the surf.

~

When I was around ten years old, my father pushed me down onto the ground so hard that my tailbone broke. He wasn't normally a physically violent person; his dissatisfaction with me or my mother usually came out verbally. This is why I know he didn't actually mean to harm me that day. I remember the look on his face when the doctor told him my coccyx was broken. He looked devastated.

We had been working on his Buick that day in the driveway. My father was a good mechanic and made a valiant effort to teach me the trade over the years. I never caught on and never cared. It wasn't my thing, but my father didn't care about that. He was determined to make it my thing. That day, I had just finished replacing the oil filter and adding oil when he had me get behind the wheel and start the engine. Not three seconds after it turned over, my father was screaming for me to turn it off. I was so startled that my hand slipped off the key at first.

"Off! *Off now!*" my father yelled as he started to lunge for the driver's side of the car. My shaking hand gripped the key and turned it forcefully toward me. The engine sputtered to a stop. I turned to face him with wide eyes.

"Goddammit! Goddammit all to hell! You nearly ruined the engine, boy!" he grabbed the creeper and rolled it partway under the car, his face red with rage. I slowly got out of the driver's seat and saw a huge, spreading pool of brown oil coming out from under the car.

"Wha...what happened?" I asked with a squeak.

"You didn't screw the filter on right. *That's* what happened!" he roared while getting onto his back on the creeper and rolling under the engine. The metal wheels pushed through the oil, leaving trails through the puddle. "The oil poured out everywhere! Jesus H.!" he continued to yell from under the car. I was so scared that I was speechless. My first reaction was defensive.

"I did! I did, Dad!" I said, even though I wasn't completely sure that I had done it right. He rolled slowly out from under the car and glared up at me. I hated the way he was looking at me. He stared at me for a good five seconds, his shoes slipping slightly in the oil.

"Don't you lie to me. I can see what happened," he said with fury. "Do you know what that could have done to the car?"

"I screwed it on, just like you showed me!"

"Obviously *not* just like I showed you!" he bellowed as he stood up and kicked angrily at the oil on the cement.

"Dad I'm sor—" I started to say, but was cut off when he stepped forward and placed his hands squarely on my shoulders and pushed me down to the ground. I felt the pain instantly, but it was overshadowed by the shock of what my father had done. My feet slipped clumsily back and forth in the oil as I tried to get up, and hot tears ran down my face. He stormed into the garage and yelled for my mother to go buy some kitty litter to sop up the oil. He didn't even go get it himself. He made her do it. They didn't take me to the doctor until the next day when the pain was so bad I couldn't sit down.

I know this memory is coming to me tonight because of the relationship I have witnessed between Dylan and his dad. It is so completely the opposite of the relationship I'd had with my father that I am fascinated by it. I had seen this father-son relationship with my friends growing up but never experienced it like this. The loving moments before bed, leaning against the father's chest as he reads, the genuine attention that Dylan is given when he speaks or learns something new. I haven't known this level of love. It makes me simultaneously resentful of, and sad for, my own father.

It's been a week, and neither Dylan nor his dad have mentioned Dylan's mother. I haven't overheard any phone calls that sound like a call with the ex-wife, but I'm also not around the dad all the time. I have seen one framed photograph on a shelf in Dylan's room: Dylan as an infant, in the arms of a woman sitting in a chair. Her face is drawn, and she looks sad. I wonder what the story is. Death, divorce, adoption, abandonment? There are no clues so far. I am just finding myself amazed at the dad who centers his life around this little boy.

As time goes on, my presence in Dylan only makes things worse for him. He talks about me more and more now, not only to his dad but also to his friends at school. I have been actively trying not to feel strong emotions. Sometimes it works; sometimes it doesn't. You can't rein in some emotions when they take you by surprise. It's an exercise in control. Today we are in hell again: day care. I didn't realize there are so many things you can do with macaroni.

While all the kids are settling down for naptime, Dylan watches as a caregiver lies down beside a little girl, talking to her softly and urging her to go to sleep. But from my perspective, something is wrong. The young male caregiver seems overly interested in the girl and is lying too close to her. My instincts flare with warning and a hot anger comes over me. I can't hold it back, and I think Dylan feels it instantly. Soon he is on his feet and walking over to a female caregiver who is washing toys in a sink.

"I can't sleep with him here," Dylan says to the woman's turned back. She turns to kneel down and face him. She looks around the room.

"You mean Gary?" She gestures to the guy that has my hackles raised.

"Noooo. The man in my head. He's angry and won't let me sleep." Dylan says this with a note of irritation, as if she should know what he is talking about. The woman's eyes widen, and she takes his hand and leads him to a bench out in the hallway. There we sit for about five minutes while she asks him questions about "the man in his head." Well let's just say the man in his head is squirming. Dylan's answers only become more and more alarming as she presses him. Oh man, this is not going to be good for him. At least he doesn't utter the typical horror-movie-with-an-evil-kid phrase: *he makes me do things, bad things.* This would rocket him into possessed-by-a-demon status. No, all he can say is that I am here, I'm always here, I'm mean and sometimes angry, and sometimes keep him up at night. Judging by the woman's questions, I can tell she is leaning toward a psychological imbalance. Better than possession, I suppose, but I still feel immensely guilty that I am having this effect on the kid. And even my feelings of guilt are probably getting through to him and only making him more aware of me.

Naturally, when Dylan's dad comes to pick him up, the woman asks to speak with him. I only hear this first part, as they are standing close to Dylan, but then they walk into an office to talk. I imagine that it starts with the usual sentence, *I'm concerned about your child*, and I'm sure most parents try not to groan at that when they hear it because they are thinking about the possibilities: fighting, not sharing, masturbating, kissing, or drawing weird pictures. Little does Dylan's dad know he will soon be wishing it was as simple as one of those issues.

After about ten minutes, they reappear and Dylan bounds up to his dad, grabs his hand, and starts pulling him toward the door.

"Let's *go*, Dad!"

I can't see his dad's face but can picture how deep the worry lines are etched in his forehead.

~

It's like torture, not knowing what the dad thinks, what the caregiver said, and what is coming next. I am reminded that children live in their own happy little bubbles and never know what is bothering their parents or what is coming next. Their own happy bubbles that is, until some weird, mean guy shows up and squats in their head. I keep waiting for the dad to say something to Dylan or ask him more questions, but everything seems normal for that evening. Then the next morning, instead of driving to the day care, his dad takes a turn onto an interstate, and Dylan notices the change of route right away.

"Where are we going, Dad?" He strains his neck to try to see out the windshield. "Are we on the wayhigh?" he asks excitedly. I see a smile come onto the dad's face.

"The highway, yes. We are doing something special today." He pauses, and I can tell he's searching for words. "We're going to see a nice lady and have a visit with her." Even from the side view we have of his face from the backseat, the dad looks uncomfortable.

"Who is she?" Dylan asks.

"Her name is Dr. Wheeler. She likes children very much and likes to talk to them. She wants to talk to you because she thinks you're interesting." The dad drums his fingers nervously on the steering wheel. Dylan thinks about it and looks out the window.

"What is enteresting?" he asks thoughtfully.

"Um, it means…neat, cool, fun to talk to."

"She thinks I'm cool?"

"Yes, definitely. And so do I."

"Am I going to day care today?"

"Nope. You won't be going today, bud."

"Cool!" Dylan starts to hum and looks out the window at the lines on the road blurring past. "I like the wayhigh," he whispers.

~

We are alone in Dr. Wheeler's office. The doctor is, no surprise to me, a psychologist. After briefly talking with his dad, Dr. Wheeler asks Dylan if it is OK if she talks to him alone. He is unconcerned and seems happy to be there. I, however, am a nervous wreck. It takes a lot of willpower not to let my emotions pour through. I am nervous, anxious, and worried. I have formed a habit of recognizing and naming emotions in a neat list, strongest to weakest. Perhaps my strongest desire, though, is to leave Dylan. That would solve this whole thing, and everything would be better for him. Dylan and his dad would go back to their normal life, and Dylan wouldn't need to see a psychologist for a problem no one else can solve. I am the cause of all this, and I feel terribly guilty. I keep questioning my existence. What is the reason for this switch? If all this is God's doing, why would God put an innocent little boy through this? But I can't say with any certainty if God has anything to do with my current existence.

Dr. Wheeler is a plump woman with a round face and kind eyes. Her brunette hair is worn in a helmet-shaped bob that is an unfortunate cut for her face shape. But her demeanor would put anyone at ease. She has a calming presence, and I feel myself relax.

"So, Dylan, what kinds of things do you like to do?" she asks with a smile. She holds no paper and pen in her lap, but has her full attention on Dylan.

"I like to build things," Dylan says. He touches a large wooden maze with balls and wire tracks that sits in front of him on the floor. He very slowly and deliberately moves a ball along the track.

"What sort of things do you like to build?" Dr. Wheeler asks. I can't see her, but can sense her leaning down from her chair toward us.

"Houses and stuff...and big cities." He cranes his neck to look up at her on the last syllable. She smiles warmly at him. These easy questions go on for a while, and I can tell she is establishing trust with Dylan. Finally, it's Dylan, not the doctor, who gets to the bottom line.

"Why am I here?" he asks sweetly.

"Well, I want to know more about the man who

visits you in your head," she replies matter-of-factly. Dylan is fully into the wooden ball maze now but looks quickly up at her.

"Oh." He pauses. "Why?"

"I think he sounds interesting. I would like to know more about him if you would like to tell me."

"Enter-esting. You think he is neat, cool, and fun to talk to, like me?" He parrots his dad innocently. Dr. Wheeler smiles, probably at what she perceives as his precociousness.

"I definitely think you are all those things. But I don't know him yet, so I just would like you to tell me about him." Her kind eyes peer into Dylan's. He sits back and looks at the ceiling as he recites what he knows about me.

"He's here." I see his hand come up to his head with what I assume is a pointed finger. "In my head, I think. He's not my friend, 'cause he doesn't talk to me. I have tried talking to him! I think he's kinda mean. He, he's…mean 'cause he's mad a lot. And I asked him to let me see him so we could play, but he doesn't let me see him." If I could have exhaled loudly, I would have. I try to control my nervousness. Dylan looks at her again. "Do you know him?" he asks her hopefully.

"No, I don't. Does he have a name?"

"I don't know," he says and returns to the maze.

"And he doesn't ever talk to you?"

"No."

"Then how do you know he's there?"

"I don't know. He just is." If I were Dr. Wheeler, I would be losing patience. But that's why I'm not a psychologist.

"Have you seen him?" she asks evenly.

"I already told you—he doesn't let me see him," Dylan says, not in a smart-ass way but in a totally honest kid way.

"OK, I forgot," she says kindly. "How does he make you feel when he's with you?"

"Hmmmmm, I don't know. I can't sleep sometimes."

"Why?"

"Just...he's there. I can...feel him. He's mad or something." Dylan is looking the other way, but I think I hear a pen scratching on paper now. Shit just got real huh, Doc? It's time to write stuff down? The next words out of his mouth stop me—and, I'm sure, Dr. Wheeler—cold.

"He's here now," he says, beginning to hum quietly as he plays.

Seemingly unfazed, the doctor says, "Did he just get here?"

"Yes."

"Is it because we're talking about him?"

"I don't know. I guess so."

"How is he making you feel right now?" she asks. Once again his eyes go up to the ceiling, and he seems to scrunch his face in thought. I see his field of vision narrow in a squint.

"Hmmmm, kinda weird." He finally settles on this adjective.

"What's weird about it?" I hear the pen scratching.

"Kinda...tight." He seems to be searching for the right words, quite understandably. How the hell does a little kid explain this?

"What do you mean by 'tight,' Dylan?" She presses him. Dylan doesn't answer right away but slows when pushing the wooden ball around. She remains quiet and patient.

"I don't know," he finally says.

"Do you mean, crowded?" Oooh, she's good.

"Crou-dad?" he asks quizzically. I've never seen a kid more interested in words than this one.

"Crowded. Like when there are too many people in a room—that makes it feel crowded. Crowded means too close to other people and you want some space."

"Oh."

"Does he make you feel like that?"

"Yeah. Too close," he mutters. The pen scratches. It hits me that she might be thinking multiple personalities at this point. Concern creeps up in me.

"Dylan, when does he visit you? Mostly during the day or mostly at night?"

"Hummm, anytime, I guess. But I don't like it when he comes at night."

"Does he ever scare you?"

"Sometimes." He says the word slowly.

"Does he give you a feeling like he's bad?" I wince, waiting for Dylan's answer.

"No..." I can tell he is thinking. "Just, like he's...sad," he finishes. I continue to be surprised at how this kid perceives me. Maybe the longer I'm with him, the better he can read me. All the more reason to vacate as soon as possible.

"Dylan, when he's with you, does he make *you* feel sad?" Dr. Wheeler inquires with a slight rise in her voice.

"Mmmm, no. I'm happy!" he says with a flick of the wooden blocks down the track.

"Good. I'm glad to hear that." I hear more pen scratching. I hope that she will rule out multiple personality disorder, but what other things will she consider? Let's hope the dreaded word "evil" is never uttered. Then our next stop would have to be a Catholic church.

"If he ever makes you feel sad, I want you to tell your dad, or me, next time you see me, OK?"

"I'm gonna come here again?"

"I would like you to, yes."

"OK," he responds. He begins to hum and stands up. He looks around the room, and his eyes land on a large, purple corduroy beanbag. He trots toward it and throws himself into it face first. The lights go out for me. I hear his muffled giggle. She's losing him.

"That's a fun chair, isn't it?" I hear her say. Dylan turns over in the beanbag and sinks back in.

"I want it!" he says loudly and looks right at her. She smiles, stands up, and sets the notepad she has been holding down on her desk. Smart cookie—she knows when to quit.

"Well, how about a sucker instead?" she asks, and Dylan practically launches out of the beanbag; for me, it feels like an amusement park ride.

"Sure!" He picks a red one from her selection and has it opened and in his mouth by the time she opens the door to escort him back to his dad. "Dad, look! It's shaped like a lion!" He runs to his dad, who is seated in the waiting area. His dad smiles widely and seems relieved. This can't be easy on him. I'm just glad what Dylan said wasn't worse. And maybe I can leave him before his next appointment. Maybe.

I'll never know what Dr. Wheeler said to Dylan's dad in the short time he spent in her office while the lady at the front desk entertained Dylan for a moment. All I know is what I saw on his dad's face when he first stepped through that door in the seconds right before he smiled at Dylan. He had the look of a man who knew he was about to go through something hard and was steeling himself against it.

~

The next week I am so on edge that it is difficult to hide my emotions from this intuitive little boy. When he feels my presence and announces it to his dad, or sometimes even to another kid, I become even more tense, and he becomes unhappy with my presence. It is a vicious cycle that will never end until I leave him. Once he started talk about me with other children, I knew things would slowly get worse for Dylan. He sounds batshit crazy when he talks about me sometimes, and I see the looks on their faces. He doesn't understand what their looks mean. But I do.

Today, Dylan's dad picks him up early from day care and tells him that we are visiting Dr. Wheeler again.

"Why?" Dylan asks.

"Because she likes talking to you and wants to see you again," his dad says, trying to sound cheerful. Dylan is silent for a while, staring out the window at a dog in the car next to us.

"She wants to talk about that man, huh," he finally says. He sounds resigned. He continues to look out the window, but I think his dad is probably looking at him in the rear view mirror, trying to gauge his reaction.

"Yes, she does, Dylan," comes the reply. Dylan is silent for several seconds. I wish I could feel his emotions.

"Dad?"

"Yeah, bud."

"Is something wrong with me?" he asks so innocently that I hurt for him. And I know he must feel it. I don't want to make it worse so I try to think about the sweet Porsche that is driving by.

"No, son," his dad says with conviction. "But something *is* happening *to* you." Dylan looks at his dad. Their eyes meet in the mirror. Then I hear the turn signal go on, and the Dad slowly moves the car across lanes, pulls over to the side of the road, and stops. Pushing the gearshift into park, he unbuckles his seatbelt and turns around to fully face us. His face is serious, yet soft.

"Dylan, I want you to know that you haven't done anything wrong. You can't help that the man is in your head. You didn't invite him. So you haven't done anything wrong, and nothing is wrong with you. You have a wonderful imagination and a big, beautiful brain, buddy. And sometimes people with big, beautiful brains have different things go on inside them. And me and Dr. Wheeler, we just want to understand what's going on in your brain, that's all. And whatever we find out, it will absolutely be OK. You understand, buddy? Whatever is going on inside your brain is going to be OK with me. You know why? Because I love you no matter what. You are special and unique, and I wouldn't want you any other way." His voice cracks on the last word, and he fights back tears. He regains his composure quickly and smiles a little at his son.

Dylan responds, with beautiful simplicity, "OK, Dad. I love you too," and starts to hum. The dad smiles more broadly and turns back around to get the car going.

My emotions hit me straight away. I feel so much—love?—for this kid in this moment that it startles me, and I almost don't recognize it. He trusts in his dad and feels safe because of him. It is as simple as that. Love can be as simple as that. I admire his dad for how he is handling a situation that could easily have damaged their relationship. This thought takes me directly to my next one: my dad. If he had only acted in my childhood just one bit like Dylan's dad, things might have been different between us. I have never felt love like this before. I have seen it portrayed in movies and TV but didn't really believe it happened. I really thought only women were capable of giving that to their children. But instead of feeling resentful toward my father, I feel a level of acceptance about who he is. He is who he is. And maybe he is that way because of the way *he* was raised, and because of *his* father. Whatever the reason for how he turned out, it is just a fact. I can deal with that fact and that he could not change it. The way he treated me in my childhood was not right. But I need to accept it, let it go, and know that right here, in this part of the world, a dad is making up twofold for my dad's shortcomings. And this is one lucky kid being raised by a single parent.

As Dylan watches a flock of geese flying in formation high above the trees, he startles me by saying, "He's happy now, Dad." His little voice fills the car.

"He is?"

"Yeah. He doesn't feel mean anymore," Dylan says and cranes his neck to watch the geese.

I feel a release within me. Relief and happiness are unmistakable emotions. I know Dylan is feeling them, and that only makes me project the feelings even more. I know what is coming. I know what will happen next. And even though I won't be here to hear it, I know Dylan will soon tell his dad he doesn't feel me anymore and that things will only get better for this pair as they go back to living a normal life in this complicated world.

12 PEACE AMONGST WAR

I arrive in my new host feeling ready for anything. Bring it on. I am just so relieved that I finally left Dylan and that I won't cause him any more psychological damage. So as the view in front of me comes into focus, I am happy to see that it looks like a relatively normal scene.

I'm in a large bedroom, sitting up in bed, watching TV. I survey what I can see of the room. It belongs to a female: lots of velvet and silk and everything in a cream, silver, and pink color palette. Then there are the perfectly polished pink toes of my host lined up and sticking out under the blanket. She isn't moving her eyes much from the TV, so I relax and try to figure out what she's watching. It doesn't take me long to figure out it's a romantic comedy, because Matthew McConaughey is in it, he is shirtless, and he just called a woman "darlin'." I decide to see if I can feel her emotions. I'm a little worried this one will be like Dylan too. But I try to relax and concentrate. One and only one emotion comes to me: content. I feel it. I feel her. Things are switched back. She feels very calm and content, and it feels nice. I would wager that most women have feelings of contentment when they watch romantic comedies. Especially those starring Matthew McConaughey.

The woman clears her throat, and sighs, leaning over to her left. Her eyes stay glued to the TV as she reaches for something. A cup with a straw comes into view. She sucks up red liquid with a long draw and then returns the cup to where she got it, all without taking her eyes off our shirtless hero onscreen. A phone rings somewhere close to her; even the ringtone is calming and suits the mood of the surroundings. Her thin white hand picks up the remote and hits pause. I glimpse matching pink polish on her fingernails. I also see blue veins straining against thin skin. She finds her phone next to her in the blankets, and I see the word "Dani" on the screen right before she answers it. She lays down on her side, and now I can see more of the room. The view outside the window on the right is distorted by rivulets of water flowing down the glass. I turn my focus to the background noise of the soft dance of rain on the roof.

"Hi, Danielle!" my host answers the phone cheerfully.

"Hey girl, how're you?"

"Oh, I'm fine. How are you? How was Aaron's spelling bee?"

"He got third place." I can hear the pride in the woman's voice.

"That's great. And what about Susan? She had a solo last Sunday, right?" The woman pulls the blanket up closer around her shoulders.

"You are sweet to remember, and yes, Susan did great, but I didn't call to talk about the kids..." Danielle trails off. When she speaks again, she sounds more serious. "How are you, Madison, really?" There is a pause while Madison stares at the water on the window, and I feel her emotions change. I believe she's nervous, but I'm still adjusting to her.

"I told you," Madison says gently. "I'm fine. I'm OK, really! I'm so tired of talking about me, though." Her voice has taken on a pleading sound. The silence on the other end lasts for just a little too long.

"OK. I get that. I was going to ask if I could come over after work. What do you think? Could you use some company?"

"Sure! But only if you promise not to give me *the look.*" I sense Madison is smiling.

"OK," Danielle says, but I hear the hesitation in her voice. "I'll be over around five-thirty, then." After she hangs up, Madison takes a deep and somewhat labored breath. She stares at the window for a while and I feel her nervousness lift when her eyes rest on an orchid plant by the window. Its large burgundy blooms look like splashes of paint against the light curtains. Her emotions return to contentment and she reaches for the remote to return to the movie.

I'll be honest. Ten minutes ago I was wondering how hot the woman in the bed is. Now, I'm wondering what might be going on with her. My guess is surgery. Or maybe grief? But that doesn't match with the feeling of contentment I am getting from her. Maybe she had a breast-enhancement surgery, and now she's feeling very content. Maybe I'll get to see them…

I snap out of my fantasy as Madison laughs at something in the movie. Her laugh is sexy and throaty, and I picture a woman tossing her long hair over her shoulder. But she only burrows deeper under the blankets. I feel her calmness again. It's tough to pin down, because it almost feels like happiness, but not quite. She seems serene yet not joyful. It's definitely a new one for me to read.

"Knock-knock," a female voice calls softly from

behind the closed bedroom door. "Come in!" Madison sits up slowly and pauses the movie.

A short woman with a soft round face and brown hair streaked with gray enters the room holding a stack of envelopes.

"How you doing, sweetie?" the woman asks. There's concern in her eyes.

"Good! You don't have to keep the door shut, Mom."

"Well, I just thought you might be sleeping, and I didn't want to disturb you."

"It's OK. I'd rather hear you puttering around the house; it makes me feel good." The woman sits down on the edge of the bed, rests her hand on Madison's leg, and hands her the stack of mail.

"Wow, a lot today!" Madison says as she looks through a stack of greeting-card-shaped envelopes. There's no junk mail or bills, just cards. I am afforded the luxury of discovering where we are by noting Madison's address: Perry, Maine. "This is so nice of people, isn't it?" She looks up at her mom who has a sad smile on her face. "Mom. You are giving me *the look* again."

"What can I get you? More water? Something sweet to eat?" Her mom busies herself with fluffing the pillows and straightening the blankets.

"Water would be great."

"With lime? Maybe some cucumbers?"

"Mmm, yes, lime. I love lime," Madison says. And I *feel* that she loves lime. I feel it. This is so cool. I stop myself with that thought. This is cool now, huh? How I have changed my perceptions.

I'm curious to see what the cards say. They will give me a clue as to what is going on with this girl and what has everyone so worried. Her mom leaves the room to get the water with the limes that inspire love. I find myself anticipating the feelings that will come with actually drinking and tasting it.

Madison looks purposefully around the room, drinking everything in. Her gaze lights upon a small throw pillow lying on the side of the bed. She tugs it over to her by its edge, and, sitting back, she examines it as if she has never seen it before. At least, she studies it for much longer than you would study a familiar object. The pillow is yellow silk, though it probably used to be white, and hand-stitched with colorful, blooming flowers in a pleasing pattern. She runs her finger across a yellow bloom, deliberately plucking at each thread carefully with the tip of her nail. I feel something from her and try to focus on and identify it. It seems...pensive, thoughtful, with a hint of melancholy. I am finding that rarely is there just one emotion at play. There are usually lesser ones hovering at the edges, waiting their turn at dominance. I am learning which emotions typically come together too, in a package deal, as it were. Pretty soon I will be a master sommelier of emotions.

The mom returns to the room with a tray holding a pitcher and two glasses, one with a straw. She sets the tray on a rolling cart and starts to pull it over to the bedside before Madison looks away.

"Ugh, please don't use that ugly thing." Madison gestures to the cart without looking at it. Her mom doesn't say a word, but I hear the cart roll away, and she places the tray on a table across the room. She fills the glasses with water and lime slices and brings them over. Madison drinks slowly, looking into the glass. When she finally lowers it, she looks right at her mom, who is waiting for her to return her gaze. Madison sighs.

"Look, Mom, it's not that I'm in denial. You *know* I'm not."

"I know you're not," her mom says. The pain in her

eyes is easy to see.

"But you should also know that I'm going to shun things that scream 'sick.' Like that over-the-bed rolly cart." Madison laughs.

"Understood. I would too." Her mom manages a smile.

"Now, let's play backgammon." Madison moves over to make room for her mom on the bed. "And if I beat you, then I'll *know* you are just treating me like a sick person, because I suck at this game." I can feel her laughter and her smile, probably before it even reaches her face.

She and her mom play the game with the ease and rhythm of those who know it well. Over and over Madison sends me feelings of contentment and calm. Their easy chat and soft voices could serve as a lullaby. They don't talk about Madison's ailment at all, but during the game an alarm goes off on Madison's phone, and her mom retrieves two pills from a bottle on the dresser. She waits while Madison swallows the pills, and then they resume their game without a word about the medicine. Madison's mom wins. I bask in Madison's own glow of losing. She is not irritated, not competitive, just…happy. I begin to wonder if the medication she is on has to do with her contented state. Is her calmness natural, or is it drug induced? Ever the skeptic, I tend to lean toward the latter. Whatever the medication, it's not like what Gwen was taking as it actually lets emotions come through. I just need more time with Madison to figure things out.

After the game, Madison and her mom open the greeting cards and read them together. There is muted scenery and pastel colors, thick cardstock with embossed flowers and birds. Brush-script font that glows gold. Every card is a somber take on "get well." The handwritten notes go far beyond the typical one or two sentences. They fill the inside of the cards and sometimes the backs. The sentiments are heart-wrenchingly sad and poignant. Some mention being friends in high school, and some are from current coworkers. There are others whose relationship with Madison I can't figure out. What I do know now is that Madison is dying.

~

Playing the board game and reading the cards seem to tire Madison, so she takes a nap, and I am left in the darkness. My mind starts to wander away to thoughts of my own life when I notice I'm seeing colors. I figure Madison is waking up, but the colors don't form into her bedroom; instead, they begin to melt into a grassy meadow. Have I jumped? I didn't experience the usual transition, but I am clearly somewhere else now. I see the green grass of the meadow lit up by sunlight. Has Madison died? Maybe she died in her sleep, and that's why I missed my usual violent transition. Maybe I am moving into the next world, whatever it is. I feel a growing elation and excitement at this new prospect. I try to feel myself in a body or move myself by free will, but I still can't. I feel like I'm floating very slowly over the ground. Maybe it is going to take a little time for me to get used to controlling my movements. Could this be it? Have I finally moved on? Did my host just have to die in order for me to do it? Sorry, Madison, but um, thank you.

I try to turn my head to look around, but I am still not in control. It is then that I notice something about my surroundings. Everything immediately in front of me is clear and sharp with color, but everything about twenty feet out is obscured by a shimmering haze that looks unnatural. And the edges of my field of vision are also hazy and fade quickly to white. But hey, who knows what heaven is supposed to look like, right? I am still floating slowly forward. The clarity of my surroundings increases directly in front of me as I draw closer, but the far-off landscape and the side views remain fuzzy. Rolling hills of green and lavender begin to show up in the distance. It is sunny out, though the blades of grass glisten as if they are wet after a rain shower. As I float along effortlessly, I suddenly find myself at the edge of a large lake. I hadn't seen it coming up in front of me, it just appears. The water is clear and an unnatural bright blue. Upon further inspection, I realize it is blue because I can see the bottom, which is entirely lined in little blue tiles, just like a swimming pool. But the shore line is edged in dirt. I peer down into the calm water, and a shape begins to form in the depths. I don't feel any fear or foreboding. The shape swims up closer to me and forms itself into a dolphin. The dolphin surfaces slowly and gently, breaking the surface of the water silently, and keeping only its head out of the water. That's when it opens its mouth and speaks.

"Hi Madison," the dolphin says in a comforting womanly voice.

Dammit. Dammit, dammit, dammit. I am still with her. I feel angry and stupid. I should have known that it was too easy. I let myself get all worked up over a false hope. I realize how odd it is to hope that I had died and moved on. But after my travels thus far, and the chaotic feel of my new "life," I want nothing more.

Madison continues to look into the dolphin's unblinking eyes. The dolphin morphs into a sea turtle. The sea turtle bobs in the water, its turquoise shell shining in the sun. I don't even feel surprised when it speaks to us.

"It's OK if you want to go."

Whoosh. The scene before me is sucked away as if

143

into a vortex, and everything goes dark; then Madison's eyes open, and we are looking at the ceiling of her bedroom. Once again I feel stupid. It was just a dream. I expect that should my host die, there would be a little more disruption or fanfare. A blinding white light, perhaps. A tunnel lined with Las Vegas showgirls. But then again, as I think back to my other visits, had I ever seen my host's dreams? I'm sure I didn't. I distinctly remember the long black nights as they slept, just listening to their breathing. I don't remember seeing dreams. Why am I seeing Madison's? How is that even possible? This is an entirely new connection.

Madison rolls over and sighs heavily, staring at the window across the room as she had before. The light of the day is fading, but not gone, and the rain has stopped. The light has that feeling of late afternoon, the way the light slants into a room as if ready to sneak away.

~

A short while later, as Madison is looking through a few celebrity gossip magazines, a creak of a floorboard in the hallway makes her look up at the doorway. A woman, probably in her early thirties, walks into the room. She looks apprehensive and is carrying a bouquet of flowers pressed tightly up against her chest.

"Hey, Danielle!" Madison throws her magazine aside.

"Hi." Her friend seems shy and comes awkwardly up to the bed holding out the flowers. I watch as her eyes dart around from Madison, to the bed, and the corner of the room where her eyes linger on something I can't see. She is uneasy.

"Oh! Thank you so much! I love Gerber daisies. You remembered that!" Madison gushes. She holds the brightly colored flowers up to her face and inhales. I felt her happiness spike.

"You're welcome," Danielle mumbles. She twists her fingers in front of her and fidgets like a child.

"Come on, sit down!" Madison urges. Danielle turns to grab a chair, but Madison says, "Oh just hop on up here. I'd rather feel like we are having a slumber party than like I'm at the hospital." I think I catch her give Danielle a playful wink.

"OK," Danielle climbs up on the bed and gets comfortable. Or, at least, physically comfortable. I suddenly feel bad for Madison. I wonder how many of her visitors act like this. But then again, how is one supposed to know how to act around someone that knows they are dying?

Danielle is damn attractive. It is nice to have someone this good looking to gaze at for a change. Despite a petite and fit frame, silky hair falling around her shoulders, and nice smooth skin, it's her eyes that I notice first, and I am captivated. They are practically turquoise. This marks the first time I have been more interested in a woman's eyes than in her body. But as Madison looks at them, I realize that Danielle is wearing colored contacts. I am supremely disappointed.

"How was work?" Madison asks her, still holding onto the flowers.

"Oh, you know, the usual. Someone in the office downloads a virus, calls me in a panic, and then won't tell me what site they were on." She laughs, and Madison joins in. "And I had lunch at that Thai place on Riven Street."

"Oh my God, yum," Madison closes her eyes in imagined bliss and all goes dark for a couple of seconds.

"Yeah, it's so good." Danielle nods but then abruptly changes the subject. She looks directly at us with big eyes. "How are you doing, Mad?"

"Oh, fine. Pretty good day overall. I've gotten my fill of celebrity trash news, though," she says as she flips a magazine further away on the bed for emphasis.

"But really, how...are...you?" Danielle asks again, and I anticipate this to be the moment in which Madison breaks down. My past experience with women says so.

"*Really*," Madison says slowly, "I'm fine."

Danielle shifts position on the bed and sighs.

"What?" Madison asks.

"Why won't you talk about it?" Danielle implores.

"Because...what is the freakin' point?" Madison says more seriously. It isn't really a question. "Because I choose not to. Because I choose to live my life the way I want, and I refuse to dwell on this one thing." She puts her hand on Danielle's hand. "I've told you this before, Danielle. I'm sorry if it makes you uncomfortable. It's what works for me," she says more softly. Danielle looks at her and sighs again. She looks resigned.

"Shit, I know," Danielle says and throws her hands up in the air. Madison laughs loudly.

"It's OK. I know it must be hard to get used to. But trust me and know that if there is something I want to talk about, or vent about, or cry about, I will just do it. I've just done an awful lot of that in the last year, and it was wasted emotion. I'm done with it."

"OK, I understand," Danielle smiles at her. "Or at least, I will try to understand."

"Thank you. So, what did you do over the weekend? Oh! I saw your Instagram post with the great new shoes. Where did you get them?" Madison leans back on the pillows and stretches her arms out toward Danielle, as if waiting to receive the gift of information.

"Oh yeah! I found them at that consignment store we went to once, the one next to the gelato place. They're vintage," Danielle says. She looks very proud of her shopping skills.

"So pretty. Who did you go with?"

"I...went with Karey." Danielle looks down at her hands and twists them in the comforter. With a tell like that, I would love to play poker with this girl.

"Fun!"

"It was OK. She's kind of annoying sometimes you know," Danielle says.

"Danielle. It's OK to tell me about hanging out with other friends." Madison's voice is soft again. She really seems to know how to talk with people. "It's not like you are cheating on me or something." She has a smile in her voice. Danielle manages a laugh.

"I know. I just...feel bad, I guess," Danielle says quietly.

"Well, I really don't want you to. I mean it. I can't do those things anymore, so you gotta do them with someone! Besides, you have to find a new permanent shopping partner anyway."

"Mad..." Tears well up in Danielle's eyes.

"Oh my gosh, stop! It's fine! You know I'm just being real."

"I know, but I'm not quite in the same place you are, acceptance-wise," Danielle says, controlling her tears and finding her voice.

"Please try to be. I've had to. I'm not trying to be harsh. I've just reached a point where reality hurts less than pretending." Madison looks down as Danielle covers her hand with her own and looks into her eyes.

"You are *so*...real. You know that? You're the most grounded person I know. And you've become even more grounded while going through this. I think you're amazing, Madison; I think you are so brave." Danielle's words all come out in a rush and by the end her voice is shaking.

"I'm not that brave." Madison laughs. "You think I

didn't go through the scared-shitless stage? You remember? I did things that reflected my fear. But it didn't feel good. It didn't give my soul peace. I finally *heard* the truth, accepted it, and promised myself I would only spend time on things that make me happy and *feed* me." They are quiet for a few seconds, and Madison looks down at their hands, still touching.

"You're fucking brave, Madison," Danielle says, and they both burst out laughing.

"Yeah. I fucking am. Now tell me, what other styles of vintage shoes did they have?" They dissolve into laughter and start talking in so much detail and with so much passion about shoes that my suspicion that women have a shoe gene is officially confirmed.

What amazes me about Madison is that through that whole conversation with her friend, as heavy as her situation is, her emotions never waver. They never take a deep dive into the depths of sadness. She maintains a neutral to happy disposition the entire time. This tells me that she really is living the way she says she is. She isn't just putting on a front or lying to herself about her positive outlook. She *believes* it. I have never known someone so in touch with herself and with such complete and utter control over her emotions. I surprise myself by finding it admirable.

~

Over the next week, I learn more about Madison and her situation. At least, I think it has been a week. It's really hard to track the passage of time while being with her. She doesn't care about what day or time it is, and there are no calendars in her room. I thought she would be on her phone more, what with all the games and apps available to entertain someone stuck in bed. But I hear her say to a friend that she has officially unplugged and doesn't care about that sort of thing anymore. She wants to read actual books, visit with people, and watch entertaining movies and documentaries, since she can't go anywhere else.

Madison has leukemia—advanced. Eight months ago the doctors gave her six months to a year of life. She is thirty-one years old and is dying from leukemia. It is heavy and awful and sad. Nurses and hospice workers visit daily. I know, and they know, and especially Madison knows, she is nearing the end. Although she is feeling worse, for the most part, she still maintains her calm and contented mood and outlook. The only times she wavers is when she is in pain. At those times I feel her resignation and her frustration, if only for a little while. There has been a multitude of visitors; everyone seems to be trying to fit in time with her while they can. It leaves her exhausted, but she is happy to see them. I see the pain and sorrow in each person's eyes as they look into hers. I don't know how Madison doesn't soak it up and feel completely sorry for herself and get depressed. But she doesn't. She reassures *them*. She comforts *them*.

I learn that she had a boyfriend, Adam, whom she broke up with a little over a year ago. They had talked about getting married. After her diagnosis, which she didn't share with him, she ended the relationship. She told him evasively that it just wouldn't work out. But really, she was just sparing him the anguish. She didn't want to put him through this. She thought it would ruin him, marrying her and getting closer and closer and then losing her. Of course, he found out through friends soon enough and begged her to come back, saying that he could take it, that he would be there for her until the end. But Madison insisted they just be friends. I learn all this straight from Madison, through conversations with friends, and with Adam himself. He has come to visit her three times in the past week. The pain in his eyes must be too much for Madison to bear. She often avoids his eyes. There are a few times when I think I sense regret from her when she looks at him. And I know I pick up on feelings of love. She still loves him. I have to question whether she helped him in the long run, or hurt him so badly that he will never recover.

Through all this, I just feel like a selfish bastard. I'm not going to lie: I keep wondering what will happen when she dies. I keep waiting to see what will happen to me. Then I feel like shit for feeling that way when a young woman is dying and so many people who love her will be sad to lose her. But I also want to know what is going to happen to me. When will this ride end? It has to end.

I hope.

~

Her suffering increases, making the days and nights long for her and for me. She frequently shivers and shakes so violently that the covers shimmy down her legs. Her mother lies with her, a cool washcloth on her forehead, and waits until the pain medication kicks in and the fever lessens. She has a cough that has worsened and often is so tired she sleeps most of the day. Visitors in her room become a blur of people and words. I hear the word "hospice" often, and many prayers are said by her bedside. Even through all this, Madison fills the few hours when she feels somewhat OK by listening to her mother read poetry aloud to her. She lets the words fill her up to the brim with contentment. Pity never enters her.

The day Madison dies, it is raining so hard I think the windows might break. It is a violent sound, a sharp contrast to the serene mood inside the bedroom. True to form, Madison has asked that everyone relax and wish her a safe journey and not cry too much or feel too sad. But she isn't really herself and isn't completely present. So she doesn't know that all the people in the room cannot fulfill that last wish. Several times someone erupts in sobs and quickly leaves the room. The pain and the morphine mix together and make her fuzzy. I can't get a read on much from her. I think I see at least ten people in the room; some are holding candles, and others have their arms around each other. Her mother is lying on the bed with her, stroking her hair. Classical music plays softly in the background, and I hear Madison mumble that it sounds nice. She had asked her mom to play it weeks ago, for this moment, always planning ahead. Her eyes soon close and stay shut for at least twenty minutes, I think. The room is quiet, yet humming with energy. I hear sniffles and whispers among the group. Then I feel my feed to her emotions stop. There is just…nothing, just a complete emptiness, and I know she has died. Life always has an undercurrent of emotion, no matter how small.

If I could have cried for her, I would have. The time I have spent with her has really gotten to me. A planned death is not something anyone really wants to witness, let alone as a completely helpless observer. I hurt for her family and friends who are left behind to grieve. I know from my short time with her that she is an amazing person that will leave a big void in their lives. I have so much respect for this woman who chose to live her life in a deliberate way after receiving a terminal diagnosis. She is likely the most self-actualized person I have ever known. And I feel changed because of what I bore witness to. The day Madison dies, something also dies in me. But it isn't a loss; it is a gain.

The first few moments after death are probably the most deeply pondered of all human wonderings. As I look into the eternal blackness after Madison dies, the anticipation and anxiousness that I feel is so intense that I can hardly stand it. For some reason I know that I won't just be going back into another person. I feel that something is different. And sure enough...nothing happens. No "whoosh" or weird sound or feeling. It just feels like when someone I'm in is sleeping. Until a voice fills the void, crystal clear, with a slight echo chasing it, "Hello?"

13 LOST

Even though I had just been with her, I am surprised to hear Madison's voice. But she sounds different. Instead of her voice feeling like it's right in my ear like all my hosts, it is separated from me, yet nearby. I still can't see anything so I wait in silence for something to be shown to me.

"Hello?" She is closer to me now. "Um, open your eyes," she says, wary. I have the distinct feeling she is talking to me. And then the second I think about opening my eyes, they are open. Madison is standing in front of me. In front of me! I stare in disbelief. She is about five feet from me, and all around us is just gray, with hardly any depth to it. I can't get my bearings. I look down and find that I actually *can* look down. I will myself to do it, and I can. I look up at Madison again. She is beautiful and has a slight glow about her. All traces of the illness are gone. In its place is the woman I'm sure she used to be. Her blue eyes sparkle and a slight smile crosses her face. She starts to look slightly amused—and hopeful.

"Are you my angel?" she asks. She sounds so

hopeful that I almost want to tell her that I am.

"No." I surprise myself by speaking. I don't even have to make an effort. The relief that floods through me at hearing my own voice is like finally getting a drink of water after crossing a desert. I raise my hands and look at them. I have my body back. I gingerly touch my torso with my hands and feel the solidness of me. In my amazement I momentarily forget about Madison.

"Who are you?" she asks, peering at me quizzically.

"My name is Cole," I whisper. I pause and realize I have no idea what to say next.

"I died, right?" Madison asks, looking confused.

"I...I'm pretty sure, yes," I say. She nods and looks at her own body, touching her hands together in front of her. She too looks at our surroundings and squints to try and see something in the gray.

"Do I...know you?" she asks. She is calm, not worried, just mystified, like me.

"No. I just...I was...visiting you for a while, I guess. Before you died." I struggle with what to say, nothing makes sense anymore. She thinks about this and doesn't seem to find it strange.

"Are you supposed to take me where I need to go?" she asks.

"Uh, I really don't know. I guess I was kind of hoping you would take *me* where *I* need to go."

She laughs softly at this. But I am starting to worry. Who is running this place, anyway? Shouldn't there be a booming voice from above and a brightly lit path showing us the way?

"Well." She smiles and looks around. "I guess we are both lost, then," she says, seemingly unaffected by the never-ending vastness. "Let's just...go," she finally says. "I'm sure whatever is supposed to happen will happen." How she can be so trusting is beyond me. I, on the other hand, have zero faith that we are on the right path. We can't even *see* a path.

This is all so surreal, but surreal has become my new normal, so I don't question it. We begin to walk. My feet touch a solid surface, but we can't even see what we are walking upon and it's very unnerving. Since there is nothing to focus my eyes on, I stare at the pattern on the flannel pajamas she is wearing. All over her back, little blue penguins hold martini glasses. This simple image calms me. It grounds me to something from the real world, at least a little. As we move forward, we reach a point where we can make out the surface below our feet. It resembles a brick path, completely smooth, and only a slightly different color of gray than the air around us. It gives us something visible to walk upon.

"So…what happened to you?" Madison asks me over her shoulder. A thousand thoughts swirl through my mind, none of them really adequate to describe what has been happening to me. So I start from what I know for sure.

"I was driving…and I guess I got in an accident, but I don't remember it. I wonder what happened to my Mercedes…" I trail off. "And the next thing I remember is being in the hospital in a coma."

"How do you know you were in a coma?"

"I could hear everyone around me, the nurses, doctors, and my parents, talking about me and my condition, but all I could do was hear. I was locked in my body unable to do anything. Not even open my eyes."

"Dang," Madison says, her eyes wide.

"Yeah. But then one day I heard the machine start beeping because my heart rate went crazy, and then it flat-lined, and alarms started going off. That's when I slipped out of my body and went…somewhere else."

"Here?" She gestures to the gray nothingness.

"No. I was, sort of, visiting people," I say. I think it's

best to keep it vague. I don't want to creep her out by describing the experiences I had been through, especially with her.

"Wow, that's kind of cool, right?" she exclaims like an excited little kid.

"Um, yeah, it was…different." I search the gray for a sign of anything around us, but there is just the brick path, barely revealing itself five feet ahead of us with every step we take. "But I guess now I get to go where we all go. I think I'm supposed to follow you."

She frowns a little at this. "Why didn't you go right after you died?" she asks. I think about this and of course don't have an answer.

"I don't know. Maybe I was supposed to visit some people on earth first."

"Oh, so they were people you knew? Those you wanted to maybe make peace with?"

"Oh, um, no. I didn't know them." I say. It sounds pathetic. Her version would make so much more sense. We are quiet for a while as we walk. It is an oppressive quiet, as not even our footsteps can be heard on the brick walkway.

"Did you see your own funeral?" she asks with much interest. "Because I would like to see mine. To see who is there, you know?" She winks at me and grins.

"No, I didn't see it; I just went straight to visiting other people," I reply. Madison considers this.

"Well, then how do you know you died?"

"What?" I turn toward her. She shrugs casually.

"How do you know you died? You only heard the flat-line. I'm sure the doctors worked on you."

"Well, we aren't at your funeral either," I say, thinking about it.

"True. But I know I died. I just *know*," she says with certainty. "Do you *feel* that you died? I mean, couldn't you still be in a coma, and your soul is out here floating around?" We are both silent for a while as I ponder this. At this point, isn't anything possible? I mentally give myself up to whatever happens. I can't worry about anything anymore. What does it matter?

"I guess I don't know that I died for sure," I admit, "but how in the hell can I find out?"

She giggles at this. "I wouldn't mention hell while we are here, you know...between worlds." She grins.

"Glad you find this so amusing. I've lost my body. Which isn't exactly on the same irritation level as losing your car keys."

Madison stops walking and looks at something out in front of her. I look too and can faintly make out something far ahead emerging out of the vast grayness.

"What's that?" I ask.

Madison doesn't answer but remains transfixed by what is emerging before us. As we watch, an archway becomes visible about thirty feet from us. As the gray air clears, it is revealed as a metal archway with vines and flowers entwined within it. It's beautiful and feels welcoming. Beside me, Madison gasps.

"It's the entrance to my grandmother's garden!" She cries with joy and disbelief. "It's what she had in her yard when I was a kid and it always had red and pink roses growing on it in the summer! I loved walking under it because I thought it was magic." She smiles in wonder and walks quickly to reach it. As we get closer the arch pulses with light and energy. The roses are blooming to perfection, and the metal gleams like gold.

"I see them," Madison whispers with wonder.

"The roses?" I ask as we stop in front of the archway.

"My grandparents," she whispers. I look but see nothing beyond or around the arch, just the endless gray. I can't see whatever she sees. I'm disappointed. This isn't for me.

Madison smiles and steps forward, slowly reaching her arms out in front of her. She goes under the arch, and I notice it pulse a little brighter in that moment. She embraces people that I cannot see. She looks so very happy and fulfilled. I too step forward slowly and approach the arch. Madison is now oblivious to me, joyfully talking to her invisible relatives. When I reach the edge of the arch, I find I can't move any farther. It's as if a force is holding me, and I can't move beyond it. I try again and even try to walk around the arch, but the same invisible force impedes me. I step back in resignation and acceptance. Madison eventually looks back at me, and the smile fades from her face. But she doesn't have to ask why I am not following her. It makes sense to us. She looks into my eyes and speaks with the reassurance of someone who doesn't entirely believe what she is saying, but wants you to.

"I don't think you're dead, Cole! If you were, you would have your own entrance here. One that makes sense only to you. You must not be dead. I think you need to find your body! It could still be in the hospital, in a coma. If you go back to it, maybe you'll wake up!"

She is smiling by the end of her pep talk, trying to make me feel better. So I smile back. But I don't even care where my body is anymore. I want to go with her. If I could stay by this amazing woman's side, I would always be led the right way and always take the optimistic view of things. That's something I never knew how to do in life. I saw how she handled death. This is someone with whom I want to enter the afterlife. But that isn't how it works, apparently.

"How do you think I can find my body?" The pleading tone in my voice surprises me. She is turning back to her family now and starting to walk slowly away from me. She is caught up in their love and embrace and can't worry about me anymore. I feel a little bit of panic rise in me. "Madison? How do you think I can find my body?" I call more loudly now, leaning as far into the arch as I can. She stops and turns halfway around, her left arm draped over an unseen person's back.

"Just focus on it, and say it," she says serenely. She holds my gaze a couple of seconds longer and then turns away and begins to walk purposefully ahead, fading into the gray. As she disappears, so does the arch. Its glow ebbs, and then the entire thing vanishes before my eyes. I am left with nothing. For about the hundredth time during my new existence, I feel utterly alone.

I stand in the emptiness and consider Madison's words. I'm also waiting and hoping that my own entrance will materialize and that it will be my turn to go. I turn in slow, hopeless circles, eyes straining in the gray, searching for any sign of...anything.

But nothing comes.

I don't know if this is good news or bad news. If Madison's theory is right, this might mean that I'm not really dead, and my body is waiting for me in the hospital. So many questions form in my mind, but I don't have answers to any of them. So I stop searching the emptiness, close my eyes, and give myself over to fate. Or whatever is in control now. I concentrate on my body. What I look like. How it felt to be in the hospital bed. I try to remember the sights and sounds there. I think about my parents at my bedside. I try to remember Kathleen Turner's voice near my ear. I take a deep breath and then say aloud, "I want to be back with my body."

For several seconds, silence presses in on me. But just when the last of my hope nearly drains, I hear a soft *whoosh,* and even feel a slight breeze and vibration. I'm not scared. I tell myself to open my eyes.

14 BIRDS AND STONES

My eyes open quickly, so I know I am of my own accord and not visiting someone else. I have to adjust to the assault of the bright light on my pupils. I instinctively raise my hand to shield my eyes from the bright sun. I am outside. As things come into focus, I see green grass at my feet and large cottonwood trees above me. I can hear birds chirping close by. I'm relieved that I'm not in someone else's body, and I come to the stunning realization that I am definitely not in a hospital room. I remove my hand from my face as my eyes adjust to the light, and I freeze at what I see in front of me.

A granite headstone stands about eight feet away. I am standing precisely facing the stone; there is no way I can miss it. I stare in shock at the intricately carved gray granite flecked with black and gold. It is wide and rectangular, curving gently along the sides. I read the words etched into the stone.

Cole M. Suter
Nov. 13, 1978–Nov. 13, 2015
May our son find peace

I read the words over and over until they blur together. I died on my birthday? And why did Mom and Dad choose those words for the epitaph? I look around the cemetery. It seems to be springtime, as the trees are only partly budded out, the grass is green, and there are only slight traces of leftover snow in the shade. If this is my local cemetery, which would make sense, I have been dead approximately five months. I have been traveling with others for five months. I am dead.

I got my hopes up with Madison and had half expected that I would return to the hospital room. I sink down to the ground and stare at my headstone. I can't feel the ground beneath me. There is no sensation. I reach out to touch the grass. My hand looks solid and real, and I can see it touching the grass, but the grass doesn't move under my touch and I cannot feel it. I look at the graves nearby. Several have fresh flowers, stuffed animals, trinkets, wreaths, and other tokens that represent the lives of the people buried here. My stone has one small bouquet of flowers that is well past its prime and half wilted, half dried. I know with certainty that the only people who have visited my grave are my parents. Of course I have no real evidence of that, but I just know it in my heart.

There isn't a woman I can think of who would come visit my grave and be sad that I am gone. I never gave any part of myself that mattered to a woman, not my mind, not my heart. I didn't have any real male friends. I used to. But I pushed them away when I became successful and wealthy and they didn't fit my lifestyle anymore. They got married and started having children. I made fun of them, was disgusted by them, and phased them out.

My colleagues were not my friends. They stopped inviting me to happy hour years ago. They stopped talking in the halls when I walked past. I had gone behind many of their backs to land a promotion and ruined their chances. I had slandered others to the executives, flat-out lying about things just to work a situation to my advantage. I remember the little seeds I had planted in others' minds, seeds of doubt that blossomed into ugly thoughts as time passed. Soon they were questioning each other, distrust growing among them, exactly as I had planned. There were the business trips to LA that involved escorts, booze, and grotesque amounts of company money spent on lobster, champagne, and room service. There was the brand-new BMW I totaled the night I was showing off to a woman I had picked up at the bar. She had a concussion and a broken wrist. She was in the hospital, and I never bothered to visit her. In fact, I never saw her again after that night. Two weeks later the company replaced my BMW with a Mercedes, no questions asked.

There is no one at my firm I can think of who would care that I had died. Not even the directors. I know they only tolerated me because I was amazing at what I did and made them richer every year. I wasn't invited a second time to an annual corporate retreat in Palm Springs after I bedded the CMO's wife in a cabana by the hotel pool. I don't think it's a stretch to say that many of my colleagues were probably secretly relieved when I died and that they struggle with feelings of guilt about being glad for someone's death. I created that guilt. The thoughts pour into my mind, and I can't stop them. I know it's the truth. I know that's how I had been. I know the truth of my life. And I would be lying if I said staring at my own gravestone with its sad and wilted flowers and remembering my life didn't make me feel deep despair.

I look up when I see people walking toward my area of the cemetery: a man and a woman, probably in their sixties, walking hand in hand in that slow way that people do in a cemetery, dreading to arrive at their destination. They come to a stop at a grave just four down from mine. I think the man glances my way, and I say "hello" out loud from habit, but they can't hear me and, of course, can't see me. I watch as they place flowers and an American flag on a small gravestone set into the earth. It appears to be a much older grave than those around it. I move closer and see the man is wearing a USMC hat, but before I even see the hat, I guess that he was once in the military. He just carries himself that way. He and the woman talk softly to the gravestone, but I can't make out what they are saying.

Just then a sparkle of light flashes in my peripheral vision, and I turn my head to look behind me. There, in the middle of all the gravestones and about twenty feet away, stands a door and frame, floating in an unearthly manner just above the ground. The door glows and pulses with warmth and welcome. I walk towards it, while glancing back at the couple. But they are completely unaware of what is happening behind them. The door is dark red with a brass knocker in the shape of a fist. It's the door from my family's first house. The one I lived in until I was seven. I had always liked our front door. Ours was the only house on the block with a red door, and I thought the brass hand knocker was something really special. That door represents the better years of my life, before my dad got mean and before I grew into the man I was. Without hesitation I walk toward it. This is my entrance. This is my turn.

15 THE CHOICE

As I come within five feet of the door, another light catches my eye. I turn to look and am surprised to see that the man standing at the grave is glowing in the same manner as the door in front of me. He has a soft, golden glow around his entire body, and as I watch, the light begins to pulse. The woman looks at him and says something but gives no indication that she can see the light around him. He puts his arm around her, and they stand still and look at the grave.

I don't know how, but I know what my choices are. I turn back to the door. I can't see what's behind it like Madison could see through her arch. And I have a feeling that once I touch that glowing brass doorknob, I will be committed to entering. I look back at the couple. The man steps slightly away from the woman, draws his feet together, puffs his chest out, raises his right arm, and salutes the grave below him. The glow around him shimmers and pulses.

I take one last look at the door and then turn and walk to the man. I wonder—what can *he* teach me?

ACKNOWLEDGEMENTS

Thank you to Julie S. for being my beta reader and for all of the mentoring, encouragement and inspiration along the way.
Thank you to Mark Finocchio, former Fire Chief, for the expertise and input.
And a world of thanks to my family and friends who supported and believed in me.